HIDDEN IN PLAIN SIGHT

Karen Ann Hopkins

ISBN: 1523947942
ISBN 13: 9781523947942
Library of Congress Control Number: 2016902625
CreateSpace Independent Publishing Platform
North Charleston, South Carolina

Praise for Serenity's Plain Secrets

"A well-crafted tale of murder begotten by the collision of two incompatible worlds." Kirkus Reviews

"*Lamb to the Slaughter* was an easy, enjoyable read that I completely enjoyed. I was over the moon excited to hear that there will be more books in this series. Serenity and Daniel will solve cases involving Amish communities throughout the Midwest!" Caffeinated Book Reviewer

"I would highly, highly recommend this one…From the mystery, the characters and the writing this is a fantastic book! I can't wait for book two!" Lose Time Reading

"From the prologue to the last chapters, Lamb to the Slaughter had me instantly hooked. Ms. Hopkins is a master at pacing and setting up her stories in a way that has readers connected to both the characters and the story line." Love-Life-Read

"This book had it all!! Murder, mystery, forbidden romance and left you needing to read the next book in the series ASAP!! Loved this book!" Curling Up With a Good Book

"Karen Ann Hopkins has delivered with Lamb to the Slaughter. I love the uniqueness she brings to the mystery genre, and I will DEFINITELY be reading more from her in the future." Unabridged Bookshelf

"The characters are complex and dimensional, whether they have a large or smaller part to play in this story, and it really added such a richness that I enjoyed." Bewitched Bookworms

"Lamb to the Slaughter is a must read for fans of mystery novels. Karen Ann Hopkins made me a fan with her YA Temptation series, and she's made me an even bigger fan with this murder mystery." Actin' Up With Books

Books by Karen Ann Hopkins
Serenity's Plain Secrets
in reading order
LAMB TO THE SLAUGHTER
WHISPERS FROM THE DEAD
SECRETS IN THE GRAVE
HIDDEN IN PLAIN SIGHT

Wings of War
in reading order
EMBERS
GAIA
TEMPEST
ETERNITY (2016)

The Temptation Novels
in reading order
TEMPTATION
BELONGING
FOREVER
RACHEL'S DECEPTION

ACKNOWLEDGMENTS

I certainly would never have seen my characters bound forever in the pages of real books without the love, encouragement and help of too many people to count, and I'm grateful to each and every one of them!

Many thanks go out to Amanda Shofner for putting her heart and soul into the edits, and to Grace Bell and Heather Miller for their amazing proofreading skills. A huge shout out to Jenny Zemanek of Seedlings Design for creating another amazing cover.

As always, much appreciation and love to my husband, Jay, and five children, Luke, Cole, Lily, Owen and Cora, for all the everyday little things and helping to make this crazy dream possible.

Many thanks to my mother, Marilyn, an avid reader of anything worth reading, who not only encouraged me to follow my dreams, but read everything that I wrote, sometimes repeatedly, and gave me her honest opinion every time.

Much gratitude to my brother, Anthony. You're always there to save the day. Thank you for everything you do for me and the entire family.

I would be remiss not to mention the wonderful Amish people who inspired me to write this series in the first place. I am humbled by the kindness shown to me and my children since our arrival in Kentucky, and I still delight in seeing the buggies whisking down the road.

> "Success is sweeter and sweeter if long delayed and gotten through many struggles and defeats."
>
> ~Amos Bronson Alcott~

PROLOGUE

November 5, 2000

The claps of thunder sent a shiver of anticipation through him. Buddy Prowes welcomed the booming noise and the spattering of accompanying rain. His booted steps on the back porch were muffled, and the flashes of light masked his shadow as he crept along the side of the house.

He pushed wet hair away from his eyes and sniffed deeply. Samantha had the woodstove stoked up and the scent of hickory burning, mixed with the dampness in the air, created a coziness that he would have enjoyed if his heart hadn't been hammering. When his fingers touched the window pane and he leaned in, he held his breath, careful not to fog up the glass.

One of the blind's panels had been bent back in the corner, and he used the resulting gap to peek in. The blue walls of his old bedroom came into view, but his gaze passed over them to settle on the bed. The covers were pushed back in disarray as though she'd just woken, but Buddy knew that wasn't the case. His ex-wife worked at one of the banks in town and would have left for work at seven-thirty in the morning and arrived home just past five o'clock in the evening, and she was compulsive about making her bed each morning. She always left the small ranch house in immaculate condition when she headed out.

His chest burned. *Sammy had someone sharing her bed.* It didn't shock him, even though the ink had only dried on the divorce papers a few months earlier. She was a beautiful woman—and a tramp. Thinking of another man kissing her plump lips and brushing his hands over her soft curves peppered his vision with purple dots.

His heart pounded as he rubbed his fist. Muted voices reached his ears, and he tilted his head to press his ear to the glass. He couldn't make out the words, but the low tone told him it was definitely a man talking.

Buddy found it difficult to breathe. Images of a stranger pressing himself into *his* woman pierced his mind, then his fist hit the wall. The conversation stopped and a moment later, the porch light flicked on.

Buddy rose to his full six foot five inches, wanting confrontation. He'd dreamed about it for weeks.

The door swung open and Samantha stepped out. Buddy noticed her bare feet first, and then how her breasts rose up and down above the flimsy nightgown with her forced breaths. But what held his attention the most was the shotgun in her hands, the barrel pointed at his gut.

"What the hell do you think you're doing here, Buddy? There's a restraining order against you. I could have you arrested for sneaking around on my porch." Samantha spit the words out, her eyes flashing.

It was her fiery temper that he loved *and* hated about her. They were two peas in a pod, a couple of wrecking balls. It made for epic sex and just as epic battles. The last time he'd seen her face to face, it had been in a courtroom and her eye had been swollen black and blue. He'd regretted hitting her and tried to explain things to the judge, but the pudgy man hadn't cared that Sammy had struck him in the stomach with a baseball bat. All his ex-wife had to do was flash her pearly whites, flip her long blonde hair and drawl that sexy voice to get her way. Buddy knew before he stepped foot in the courtroom that he'd been a fool to think he had a chance of winning.

His mouth twitched. "This is my damn house and you're fucking some other man in there." He thrust his hand at the window. "This ain't right, and you know it."

Sammy's eyes narrowed. "We're divorced. I got this dump and you got the pickup truck." She dropped her voice, and it occurred to Buddy that she didn't want whoever was in the house to hear her. "I can fuck whoever I want now."

The words and the curl of her lips were too much. Buddy rushed forward, only stopping when the barrel of the gun jabbed into his chest.

"Come one step closer and I'll blow a hole in your heart. I swear I'll do it."

The glint in her brown eyes confirmed her threat was real. Buddy hovered over her on the balls of his feet. His heart pounded in his ears. *Even if she gets a shot off, I'll still be able to grab her neck and squeeze—squeeze the life right out of her.*

He pressed against the gun and smiled at Sammy. "You're nothing but a whore and not worth a hole in my gut, or worse yet, a prison sentence." The corner of his mouth lifted higher.

"But we aren't finished with this conversation. Not by a long shot."

He swiped the gun sideways and took the porch steps two at a time until he reached the gravel driveway.

"You better stay away, Buddy Prowes, or I'll kill you myself," she shouted after him.

Buddy darted into the trees, taking the packed dirt path he knew so well. It led to other trails, some that went deeper into the woods and one that skirted the road to where his truck was parked. He turned to the right, away from the road, heading in the direction of the creek bed and his old deer stand. The rain became a drizzle and the flashing storm moved off to the east. He held his face up to the cold wetness, gulping for air.

When he reached the poplar tree with the ladder made of wooden boards, he paused to catch his breath. The fast-moving clouds occasionally allowed light from the full moon to shine through the tree branches, lighting the forest floor with a dappling effect.

He squatted beside the tree and ran his hand through his reddish beard with a tug. He had half a mind to slip back to the house and teach Sammy a lesson right then and there. Whoever had been with her had probably already slipped out the side door. She was delusional if she thought she could have another lover while he was still breathing. He'd never allow it. But if the man who'd been with her was foolish enough to have stayed, his truck would still be parked on the road, just where Buddy had seen it earlier.

He chuckled, and his breath puffed in the cool, damp air. He straightened, eager to make his way back, with a plan that lifted his spirits. He'd get the truck's license plate number, and one of his friends in the sheriff's department would run the plate number and give him the name of its owner. He'd make sure the new boyfriend was out of Sammy's life, one way or another.

A smile curled his lips as he pushed away from the tree, but it was replaced with a frown. He stopped.

He peered into the shadows, shifting his head to listen better. "Who's there—Sammy is that you?"

Buddy's chest shuddered out of his chest as he squinted into the darkness. The clouds parted and moonlight illuminated the trees. He exhaled, his shoulders slumping. "Oh, it's just you. It ain't wise to sneak up on a man like me in the dark. You ought to know better."

He saw the gun right before it fired. The explosion echoed in his head and the force that smashed into his stomach knocked him backwards into the tree. He pushed his hand inside his coat flap and felt a sharp pain in his gut and a sticky wetness on his fingertips.

"Dammit, you done shot me," he croaked. His legs buckled.

The moonlight disappeared behind the clouds, turning the forest dark again. Except for the soft pattering of rain and his sharp breaths, all was quiet. Buddy was numb. He struggled to keep his eyes open as the blood pumped freely out of the gaping wound.

He felt as though he were floating under water, tipping and sinking.

He blinked and blinked again.

An ax rose high in the moonlight before it came down on his head.

1

May 12, 2015
Blood Rock Amish Settlement

I had a moment of déjà vu as I lifted my face to the warm
sun, closed my eyes and inhaled the smell of churned
dirt. My heart sputtered. Only seven months had passed
since Naomi's body had been discovered, shot and decayed
in the cornfield, but a lot had happened since then. When
I'd started that investigation, I had little experience with
Amish people. Now, after several cases in my own jurisdiction
and across state lines, I was all too familiar with the secretive
culture.

"Ma'am, do you think this guy will even talk to us?"

I looked over at U.S. Marshal Toby Bryant. His cowboy hat
shielded his eyes from the glaring sunlight, giving me only a
glimpse of his bright blue eyes and lopsided smile before he
glanced away. His gaze followed the same direction of his partner, John Ruther, who shaded his eyes with his hand. John was
the older, more laid-back of the pair. His tie flapped in the wind.

I resisted the urge to groan and rubbed the side of my leg, scratching at the healing wound I'd suffered when a house had exploded on top of me a few weeks earlier. It was a miracle I hadn't been more seriously injured. A boy and a woman had died in the incident. Eli, I mourned, but Ada Mae had gotten what she deserved. But dammit, if the itchy-soreness of my leg wasn't a constant reminder of that day.

"We're the same age and rank. Call me by my name," I said.

John laughed. "You'll have to excuse Toby. He was born and raised in Oklahoma. It's his custom to be annoyingly polite."

I smiled behind my hand. It was nice to have someone agree with me for a change. I turned back to the cowboy. "To answer your question, I have no idea. The Amish are unpredictable people. Sometimes they don't stop talking and other times they won't say a word." I shrugged. "I guess it depends how close to home this case is for them."

"Is that their bishop?" John pointed at the silhouette of a four draft horse team and a man standing on the plow behind them in the distance.

I nodded. "I appreciate you giving me time to get back on my feet before we came out here, but you still haven't explained exactly why you're here. Mind letting me in on some of the details before he reaches us?"

John and Toby exchanged glances. John answered, "Some fifteen years ago, a fellow marshal by the name of Jim Allen worked a case in Pennsylvania. It involved a man who was shot to death and then bludgeoned with an ax. The crime was especially horrific given the overkill nature of it. Local law enforcers bungled the case, being overly zealous to pin the crime on someone."

"Sounds complicated," I commented.

John snorted. "The vic, Buddy Prowes, was a favorite of the good ol' boys' club. He was one of those types who got away with behavior that would have put most people in jail, because he'd grown up with the same crew that ran the town. He had a list a mile long of complaints against him, everything from domestic abuse towards his wife to assault on neighbors."

My eyes widened beneath my sunglasses and Toby kicked a clump of dirt with his cowboy boot. He bumped his hat back and looked at me. "A real A-hole type."

"Okay, so the guy probably deserved what he got. Were there any other crimes connected to the case?" I asked, pushing the stray hairs escaping my ponytail behind my ear.

John shook his head. "No. It was personal."

"So why your interest in a cold case—what's changed?"

John took a step closer toward me. The team of horses was close enough to hear the jingling of their harnesses when he spoke. "Jim passed of cancer last month. This case was his Achilles' heel—you know, the one he couldn't get out of his mind all these years—the unsolved mystery." He leaned in closer. "I received a package from his wife, Stephanie, about a week after he died. It was the Buddy Prowes' case file. Jim had written some new notes—information he'd collected recently, before he'd gone into hospice." He pulled a piece of folded paper from his inside jacket pocket. The paper was rumpled, old looking. "He'd gone over the papers he'd received from local law enforcement a hundred times or more, never coming up with anything fresh—" he unfolded the paper and thrust it at me "—then he had a break through."

I scanned the handwritten note, pausing on the writing in red ink. *Bloody Rocks—Blood Rock. Amish.* Amish was underlined in a darker scribble. I looked up.

"Jim had assumed these notes, taken at the scene by a deputy, who was later killed in motorcycle accident, meant the rocks around the body were bloody. There had been testimony by one of Buddy's coworkers about Amish boys working on the crew. Jim visited the neighboring Amish settlements, but never came up with anything. Recently, a woman approached him with new information. Stephanie mentioned to me that her husband had gone back to one of those communities after he spoke to the woman, and it was then—" he touched the words *Blood Rock* with his finger "—he realized that he'd misconstrued the meaning of these words. Jim had also scribbled the name, Jerimiah Suggs on the backside of the file at some point."

"This is all you have?" I handed the paper back to him.

"I believe the person who killed Buddy was from this community…and there's a good chance he came back here after he did it." John stared at me as though it was a challenge.

I glanced at Toby and he grinned back. "What better place to hide than among a group of people who all blend together in dress and manner and live so secretively?"

He had a point, but it still seemed like searching for a needle in a haystack. And if we did find that needle, more than likely I'd be the one getting poked by it.

One horse whinnied and another snorted when the team stopped alongside us. Giving some authenticity to Toby's dress, he stepped up to the nearest horse and patted its sweaty neck.

John hung back, looking behind the horses at the Amish man holding their reins. He was tall, wiry thin, and sported a long, bushy white beard. His suspenders hung loosely at his sides and his sleeves were rolled up to his elbows, revealing jagged, red scars from shrapnel that had hit him in the same house explosion that injured my leg. His hat was a simple straw one, and beads of sweat dripped down the sides of his face. His white brows were equally thick, but his nearly black eyes squinting at us were the most startling aspect of his appearance.

My mouth dropped at the sight of him in such a casual and messy state. Whenever I'd seen him in the past, he was always smartly dressed in a black hat and coat that made him look even more intimidating.

"Well now, what brings Blood Rock's sheriff out into my cornfield on such a fine day—and accompanied by guests?"

I wasn't fooled by his friendly tone. His eyes passed over the marshals, landing on me. A single brow arched and his lips tightened.

Aaron Esch wasn't a happy camper.

2

"Good morning, Bishop." I flicked my hand at the marshals. "This is John Ruthers and Toby Bryant. They're U.S. Marshals working a case that's brought them to Blood Rock." I took a quick breath. "Do you know anyone by the name of Jerimiah Suggs?"

The bishop pursed his lips and scratched his chin through his thick beard. His facial expression confirmed he was speaking the truth when he answered, "No, I don't recall the name. Suggs isn't an Amish surname."

"No, it isn't," I agreed. "Perhaps you remember an Englisher by the name?"

He shook his head. "Not off the top of my head." He took a step closer, ignoring John's and Toby's curious gazes. "We've had enough tragedy lately to last a lifetime. The community is still recovering from Eli's and Fannie's deaths, and Ada Mae's sins." His brows scrunched. "Surely, these men don't come bringing more hardship to my people."

I licked my dry lips and glanced at John. He took the cue and reached out his hand to the bishop, who took it in a firm handshake. "It's a pleasure to meet you. Toby and I aren't here to cause you any undue duress, I promise." He exhaled, looking at one of the horses when it stomped its foot. I thought the marshal was taking the unorthodox location of the questioning well. "We're working a cold case…regarding a murder that took place about fifteen years ago in Clay, Pennsylvania—"

"That's the northern part of Lancaster County, is it not?" the bishop interrupted.

"Yes, as a matter of fact it is—not too far from one of the largest concentrations of Amish people outside of Ohio, and of course, here in Indiana." John paused, tipping his head sideways.

"Was the murdered person one of my people?" the bishop asked.

John shook his head. "No—he was builder though, and it was brought to our attention he had a few Amish lads on his crew at the time of his death." John's brows arched. "Because of the secrecy in the neighborhood, it was difficult to get answers about the boys. As a matter of fact, after Buddy Prowes' death, they disappeared into thin air."

I broke in. "You weren't able to identify everyone on the vic's crew?"

"No, and believe me, we tried." John turned his attention back to Aaron, and I rubbed my forehead, pressing into the thrumming of a beginning headache.

I sympathized with the marshals. I knew firsthand how incredibly difficult it was to investigate a crime inside an Amish community. The culture was not only secretive, but it had an element of vigilantism I'd learned about on my first murder case in Blood Rock, too. The Amish protected their own—but they punished them as well.

I saw the hint of a smile creep onto the bishop's mouth, then it was gone. "I don't see why you're seeking me out. I've lived in this settlement for nearly forty years. Close to the time of this murder you're talking about, I took the reins of bishop here. I don't know anything about the crime."

"But you have visited Lancaster County on occasion, haven't you, Mr. Esch?" Toby spoke up for the first time. It wasn't lost on me that he didn't address Aaron with his religious title. "And there have been youth from Blood Rock who've traveled to Pennsylvania to work or socialize throughout the years?" he added.

The bishop shrugged. "For many of our young people, visiting other communities is part of growing up. As you said, they may travel to find work, but most often it's to stretch their wings a bit and meet a suitable mate." He smiled. "It's one of the reasons our people have been moving into new areas, expanding our borders. We understand the need for our children to spread out and meet people who aren't related too closely to them."

The conversation had taken an uncomfortable turn and I glanced away, staring down the newly tilled row. The smell of worms and dirt was heavy in the air, and as the sun rose higher in the sky, it became warmer. I shifted to allow a little more ventilation under my arms. Even with copious amounts of antiperspirant, it was impossible not to sweat in my black uniform jacket.

"Some new information came to light that led us to believe that one or more of those boys may have been originally from here." John's face hardened. "Do you keep any kind of records of who comes and goes in your community?"

The bishop barked out a laugh. "No, no. There are no records for such things. I'm afraid I can't help you, Marshal."

John was about to speak when I touched his arm. "It's all right. We understand." I tipped my hat to the bishop. "We'll get out your hair so you can finish plowing."

He looked back at me with a raised brow before he turned away. He'd only taken a couple of steps when he stopped and looked back over his shoulder. "If any memories strike me, I'll contact you, Sheriff."

"Thank you." I motioned for the marshals to follow me back to my cruiser. Once we were seated in the car with the air conditioning blasted, I dropped my head back. "You didn't actually think he'd come up with names and numbers for these boys you're looking for?"

John grunted and wiped his forehead with a handkerchief. "I believe we're going to have a hot summer," he said, almost to himself, then added, "There has to be a way to track the boys, find out who they were and hopefully even talk to them."

"Oh, there is, but I have to ask, do you think an Amish boy, or group of them, murdered Buddy?"

John's face scrunched. "I've learned through personal experience that anyone is capable of murder." Our eyes met, and I knew we understood each other perfectly. "Where do we find our answers, Sheriff?"

"A good place to start is with my boyfriend." John's eyes widened, and I added, "He used to be Amish."

John and Toby stood beside me as Daniel climbed down the ladder leaning against the house. He wore a gray t-shirt and blue jeans that hugged his butt. The jingle of tools on his belt didn't distract me from noticing his bulging muscles. Heat fanned my cheeks and I hoped the marshals didn't notice. Being around Daniel turned me into a hormonal teenager, even though we'd been dating long enough that his handsomeness shouldn't affect me anymore. It was one of the reasons the relationship bothered me. I didn't like the feeling of wanting someone so much it hurt. It made me vulnerable, and that was a place I didn't like to be.

His feet touched the ground and he strode over, wiping his hands on the sides of his jeans. "What's going on?" He frowned at me before shifting his eyes to the marshals. He extended his hand to John. "It's good to see you again. Marshal Ruthers, right?"

"Good memory." He nodded to his partner. "Toby Bryant."

Daniel continued to look anxiously at me and I smiled in an attempt to ease his worry. I could hardly blame his reaction. Usually when I showed up unannounced at his workplace, someone was dead.

"Mr. Bachman—" John began.

"Call me Daniel—Mr. makes me feel older than I want to be." He smiled tightly.

John nodded briskly. "The sheriff was telling me you used to be Amish and grew up in the Blood Rock community."

"Yes, I did, but it's been a long time. I'm probably not a very good source of information for a cold case investigation."

John ignored him. "We're interested in the time period around 2000."

"I left the Amish a year earlier—went English. I'm sorry, but I didn't have anything to do with the community until just recently." He leaned in, lowering his voice. "My folks took the shunning thing seriously."

John's stance softened. "I can only imagine what that's like."

Daniel looked away. I knew how difficult it was for him to talk about the first years after he was shunned. I cleared my throat. "Who can we talk to who might actually help us out on this? A man was brutally murdered—we need some answers."

His lips tightened and he blew out a breath. When he looked back, he was thoughtful. "You might try my sister, Rebecca. She likes you, Serenity—you saved her little girl twice, she might give you some information."

Toby's brows rose and I wagged a finger at him. "It's a long story. Are you boys up to driving back to the community this afternoon?"

"Absolutely," John replied. "Your ties to the Amish in this area are giving us more opportunities than we had back in Lancaster."

I grinned. "I guess you can say I've been sucked into their intrigue on both a professional and personal level." My stomach growled and I hoped no one heard. "But first, why don't we get some lunch? There's a diner in town with excellent bacon cheeseburgers." My smile deepened. "It will give us the opportunity to go over the case, and for me to look through the file Jim put together."

John and Toby exchanged glances. I could see the wordless exchange between the two. The cowboy was more relaxed than John, who was older and did things by the book. He didn't seem so sure about sharing information.

After an awkward pause in conversation, Toby spoke up. "Sounds wonderful, Sheriff. I'm so hungry I could eat an entire cow."

"Then Nancy's is the place for you." I looked at Daniel. "Do you want to join us?"

"Naw. I've got a couple of new crewman I should keep an eye on. It's supposed to rain tomorrow. We have to finish this roof."

I stared at Daniel through my sunglasses. What he said seemed perfectly reasonable, but I still didn't like being blown off. He wasn't a lawman, although he'd helped me with several investigations regarding the Amish. I got the impression from his rigid posture that he felt left out of this one.

"I'll see you for dinner?" I asked.

"Of course." He bent down and planted a firm kiss on my lips, before nodding to the marshals and heading back to the ladder.

The kiss and the promise of dinner lightened my mood, but when I saw the smirk on the cowboy's lips, I bristled. "We all have personal lives."

Toby snorted and flicked his thumb at John. "Not with this partner—no personal life here."

John rolled his eyes. "There's time for a life later, after the case is solved."

"That's why you're fifty-something, never married and no kids—there's always another case," Toby snickered.

We walked back to the car in silence, but when I grasped the door handle, I stopped and looked at John. "Sometimes, in this line of work, all we have is today."

"Well said," Toby replied before ducking into the back seat. He winked at me, but he wasn't smiling. He was all too aware that in this business, any day might be our last.

3

I scanned the death report again and then dropped it on the table to take a sip from my cola. Toby and Todd conversed in hushed tones about the armed robbery that had taken place several weeks earlier at the bank across the street from the diner. John met my gaze when I looked over.

"I didn't see any mention of Jerimiah Suggs anywhere else in the file, other than scribbled on the back of it, like you said. You couldn't find anyone in the area by that name?"

John shook his head. "We came up empty."

My eyes drifted to the window and the sunny street with men and women bustling about in their business clothes. The town and the Amish settlement were remarkably quiet, making me wonder if something bad was about to happen. I'd learned the hard way that tranquility didn't last long around here.

"Did you consider that he jotted the name down for an unrelated matter—maybe he needed something to write on and the file was the only thing available?"

John chuckled. "That would be something, wouldn't it? He drew in a sharp breath. "Jim was a meticulous kind of guy—and he knew he was dying. He would've been careful to cross out the name if that were the case. Since he didn't, I assume he felt it was important enough to remember."

"The brutal nature of the attack points to it being very personal." I met his steady gaze. "This wasn't a random killing. The perpetrator had a close relationship with Buddy."

John swirled his finger around the rim of his iced tea. "I agree, and so did Jim. He interviewed family members, close friends and the coworkers he could track down." He lifted a brow and shrugged slightly. "Buddy was one of those people you either loved or hated. There wasn't much of an in-between with him."

"He had enemies?"

"Sure, too many to count, but he was a big, burly man, known for a foul temper and violent episodes. Most people didn't mess with him."

Tony Manning, the former Sheriff of Blood Rock and my nemesis, popped into my mind. "Yeah, I know the type. What about relatives? What was his personal life like?"

"He was recently divorced at the time of his death. The investigation turned up leads to several men, who his ex—Samantha Prowes—might have been sleeping with, but nothing concrete. Sammy was known to have a hot temper herself, but she usually ended up more battered than he did."

"It says here—" I shuffled through the papers until I found the right one "—she had a restraining order against him and yet he was murdered only two hundred yards from her house." I leaned back in the booth. "I think it's fairly safe to assume there's a connection."

"Jim thought so, but never had a breakthrough in that direction." John's eyes flicked up at Nancy when she appeared at the end of the booth, balancing a tray filled with our orders.

Todd pushed his cola out of the way for Nancy to have room to deposit his plate. "Looks like the lunch rush hour began early this morning," he commented, plucking a fry off his plate and popping it into his mouth.

Nancy placed the remaining orders in front of us and bent over the table. She jerked her head towards a booth closer to the stool-lined counter. "There's a new Amish fellow in town." She lowered her voice and glanced over her shoulder. John gazed up at the redheaded woman expectantly. "Joshua Miller is his name. He's a dreamy one. They're having some kind of meeting over there."

I elbowed Todd to lean further back so I could see around him. Nancy wasn't lying about the newcomer's good looks, but my gaze didn't stay with him for long. My body tensed and my blood turned cold when I saw who he was sitting with.

"Thanks for pointing him out to me, Nancy." I turned back to John and Toby who sat across the table. "If you'll excuse me for a moment."

"Of course," John said. Toby's brows arched and Todd rolled his. My deputy officer had the same reaction whenever anything with the Amish came up.

I slid past Todd when he stood and stepped out of the booth. Nancy sidled up to me and whispered, "Should I prepare for some excitement?" She spoke cheerfully, but the twitch at the corner of her mouth told me she was concerned.

I placed a hand on her shoulder. "No worries. Just a friendly chat."

Elayne Weaver was the first to spot my approach. Her pretty face lit up. "Serenity, it's good to see you. I heard you were back to work—I meant to stop by your office last week, but I've been so busy getting settled into the new job."

Even though we'd made our peace, the assistant DA's feminine, overly perky voice grated my nerves. The fact that she used to be Amish and had a crush on Daniel when they were teenagers didn't help either. No matter how much I tried, I couldn't stop a knot from forming in my stomach every time I saw her.

"I've been busy too," I said.

The brunette peeked over at my booth and her smile diminished. "Looks like it."

Before she had a chance to turn the tables and question me about my guests, I eyed Moses Bachman, Daniel's father. "Hello, Mr. Bachman. I wouldn't expect to see you in town having lunch with the assistant DA and the former sheriff of Blood Rock."

Moses' cheeks reddened, but he didn't get a chance to respond.

"Moses and I go back a long time, as you already know." Tony Manning smirked. "It's a free country." He popped his neck, making a loud enough crack for everyone to hear. "This time of year, Florida gets a little too steamy for comfort, so the wife and I came north for the summer." He smirked again, his crystal blue eyes sparking with challenge. "Nothing better than spending the winters in the south and summers in the north. Perhaps you'll be so lucky, Sheriff."

Visions of the man standing over me in a dark barn and kicking my stomach were still fresh in my mind. And I was certain he'd been the one who'd set my house on fire when I'd pried into his past and his relationships with the Amish authority. He'd gotten off easy because the DA and Mayor were his friends, and I was a newcomer. I was still bitter about it and what I really wanted to do was leap into the booth and punch his smug face.

I was good though. Tony was goading me and I knew it. He would like nothing better than for me to attack him in plain view of everyone. He probably had some delusion about getting his job back if I did. I caught a glimpse of Todd across the diner. He stretched out of our booth, observing the scene with wide eyes, looking like he was prepared to rush forward if I needed him. Or maybe he was planning to stop me from killing the former sheriff in front of half the town. Either way, Todd was a solid partner. He always watched my back.

I forced a confident smile. "I like the snow too much to leave in the winter." I dismissed Tony Manning and settled my attention on the man seated beside Elayne.

She took the cue and spoke up. "This is Joshua Miller." As if she was attempting to smooth over being caught with Tony Manning, she volunteered more information. "He's moving here from Pennsylvania—" she gestured across the table at Moses and Tony "—and buying some combined land from them, along with Jonas Peachey's farm."

My face twisted at the news and Elayne hurriedly said, "I'm doing some real estate law on the side. Because of my former connection to the Amish community, I'm handling their closings."

I wasn't as concerned with Elayne's involvement as I was with the fact that Jonas was selling his farm. He was a medicine man—a legitimate one. I'd seen his work firsthand, in both the medicinal and spiritual realms. I never used to be a believer in magical, miraculous healings, but I was now. He was the real deal, and he had been the number one suspect in a series of childbirth deaths among the Amish on my last case. It turned out his sister, Ada Mae, had been the one poisoning the victims, and Jonas had been exonerated of all crimes except fooling around with a slightly impaired young woman in another community. There weren't any laws against being a jerk in this country.

"Is he moving back to Ohio with his girls?" I asked.

Moses answered, "We decided as a community that it was better for Jonas to leave. He's returned to his previous home with his youngest daughter, Esta. He has family there to help him raise the child. Verna, the elder, remained here and is staying with Anna and myself." Seeing my brows shoot up, he explained, "Jonas is Anna's distant kin. We felt it was our duty to take the girl in so that she and Mervin could continue courting." He scratched the side of his face. "Having a youngster in the house has been trying." He shrugged. "But Anna's enjoying the company."

I snorted in my mind. I was sure it had been Daniel's mother who'd insisted on having Verna stay in their home. In most respects, the men ruled within the community, but there were times when the women showed strength and got their way. Courtship matters were probably one of them.

Elayne spoke up. "It's customary for young people to sometimes live in a community away from their parents during the courting process."

Mervin was only sixteen years old. His brother had shot and killed Naomi Beiler out of cold-blooded jealousy because she didn't return his favor, and he was now in a mental institution for the crime. His mother had tried to cover up the murder to protect her son. Verna's family history wasn't much better. Her aunt had killed her mother and a local girl through poisoning and struck a lighter after she'd purposely flooded a house with natural gas, causing an explosion that killed young Eli Bender, as well as injuring me and the bishop. To say Mervin and Verna were probably in for a bumpy relationship was putting it mildly, but their tender ages bothered me the most. They were still kids.

But the sun was shining brightly beyond the diner's window, and it was difficult to stay immersed in dark thoughts. I swallowed, turning my attention to Mr. Miller. I reached my hand out. "Welcome to Blood Rock." I tried to keep my voice level. "What part of Pennsylvania are you from?"

"Lancaster. Moses is my uncle and he's been generous enough to arrange the sale of the properties for me so that my family can move here."

"How does your wife feel about relocating?" I studied Joshua's face closely. He appeared to be in his mid-thirties—the same age range that an Amish youth who worked on Buddy's work crew fifteen years ago would be. His gray eyes were hard, giving me the impression of a man who didn't let many people in.

"My wife passed away last year. I'm here with my children and my grandmother, who helps care for them."

I immediately thought of Rowan Schwartz in the Poplar Springs settlement up north. He too had lost a young wife and put in charge of raising the kids. It seemed to be a common theme among the Amish nowadays.

Elayne frowned up at me and Moses looked away. Tony continued to smirk. I straightened and smiled politely. "Good luck to you, Joshua." I glanced at Elayne. "I'll touch base with you later this week. Enjoy your lunch."

When I sat down beside Todd, I took a bite out of my sandwich and chewed. He looked sideways at me with raised brows while the marshals watched me in silence.

I swallowed. "Is Jerimiah Suggs the only name you have that isn't matched to a person?"

John crossed his arms and nodded.

"We'll find him—and the mysterious Amish boys," I reassured him.

Toby laughed. "Sounds like we have ourselves a new partner, John."

John cleared his throat. "Perhaps a temporary one. We owe it to Jim and Buddy to solve this one. I'm willing to step outside of protocol to get the job done."

"I think we're going to get along fine, marshals." I took a sip of cola.

Todd shot me the *Oh, no, not again look*, but I ignored him. I was enjoying the pounding rhythm of anticipation in my gut too much to let him dampen my mood.

4

Rebecca struggled to pull a pair of soaked navy blue pants through the old-fashioned wringer, and then dropped them with a wet *kersplat* into the laundry basket with the others. Without missing a beat, she snatched another pair out of the tub filled with the rinse water and squeezed it with her hands to get rid of the excess moisture before she fed it through the wringing contraption that didn't seem to work properly.

The process of doing laundry for an Amish woman was lengthy and tedious. My gaze shifted to the piles of towels, dresses and boy's shirts separated neatly on the basement floor. Rebecca's older daughter, Sarah, heaved up the heavy basket with the damp pants onto her hip and made her way out the doorway to the waiting clothes line. Water dripped in a steady stream from the basket as she crossed the basement floor. The front of her dress was soaked and yet she was still smiling as she worked. It was hard to believe the teenager was Daniel's niece. Sometimes when I was with him, I completely forgot about his upbringing. Then I'd have moments like this, where I realized these were his roots, and it startled me.

Christina giggled, drawing my attention away from her older sister. Her sleeves were rolled up to her elbows as she swirled the towels in the sudsy water. The strong scent of bleach made my eyes sting and I cringed at the sight of a six-year-old child submersing her bare hands into the water.

I wrinkled my nose and turned away. *This is their culture— they're okay with it and so is the government, so it's none of my damn business*, I told myself for the hundredth time. By the look of horror on John's face, he agreed with me, but Toby was too busy studying the gas pipes connecting to a refrigerator setup in the corner to pay any attention to the work the small child was doing.

Toby coughed to get Rebecca's attention. "Are all of your appliances powered by natural gas?"

She stopped tugging on a fresh pair of pants. "Mostly. For some things we use batteries—" she tilted her head towards the wringer "—and others, we do it ourselves."

"I'm sorry we came at a bad time," I offered, but Rebecca shot me a frown and shook her head.

"You're welcome anytime, Sheriff." Her lips pulled back up and I saw a glimpse of Daniel in her features. "Besides, catching me when I'm not doing laundry, gardening, mending or preparing supper is difficult indeed."

I couldn't stop myself from commenting, "It's a hard life."

She dropped the last pair of damp pants into the basket waiting in Sarah's arms, who'd quickly returned from the clothes line. "Keeping busy is a good thing. From what I've seen of your life, you're going nonstop as well, just not the same kind of duties."

I caught Toby wiping the smile from his face as he stepped up. She was right, in a way.

"Here Mamma, let me and Christina finish up here. You go talk to the sheriff." She glanced at me. "I'm sure our laundry duties are putting them to sleep."

Daniel's niece looked to be about sixteen with the same dark hair as her uncle and mother, but where their eyes were brown, hers were sparkling green, like fresh cut grass. She appeared to be a dutiful Amish girl, but I sensed a reckless spirit inside of her. Her suggestion to her mother showed a sharp mind, too.

Rebecca reached for a towel on the counter and dried her hands. She said a few words to Sarah in Pennsylvania Dutch, a language I still hadn't picked up, except for a few words and to know that it was a mixture of the Dutch and German languages with a few English words thrown in.

We followed Rebecca up the stairs and back into the sunlit kitchen that smelled like fresh-baked cookies. I inhaled the pleasant aroma and took a seat beside Toby at the table. John sat across from us. Rebecca insisted on pouring us cups of tea after she placed a plate of snickerdoodles between us.

John passed on the cookies, but Toby didn't hesitate snatching one up. I nibbled mine, any angst about a six year old doing laundry by hand in this day and age evaporating. As long as the Amish were content with their way of life and kept on cooking and baking the way they did, little else mattered.

I spotted a quilt spread out on the frame in the adjoining room. It was all shades of blue, with pieces of floral patterned triangles woven into the design.

"Are you making that quilt with your girls?" I asked.

She shook her head. "Several other women in the community, including Ma and Katherine, are helping. It'll be auctioned at the summer benefit dinner for the schoolhouse expenses," she replied, taking the seat at the head of the table.

The cookie turned to chalk in my mouth. Katherine was the one Amish woman who I'd bonded with, and she was also Eli's grieving mother.

"How is Katherine doing?" I looked away and back again. "I wanted to check in on her, but wasn't sure if she was ready for visitors."

A few strands of Rebecca's hair had escaped from her white cap and she stuffed them back in. "She's putting on a show for everyone else, but I know she isn't recovered. I don't think losing a child is something a mother ever gets over." Her gaze became moist. "I'm sure she'd welcome a visit from you, though. Everyone in the community is grateful for what you did for Hannah and how you exposed Ada Mae's sins." She reached over the table and patted my hand. "You can't save everybody, Serenity."

I forced myself to swallow down the burning sensation in my throat. I wasn't an emotional person and I was careful to hide my thoughts from others, but Daniel's sister had read me like a book. On a mental level, I knew there was nothing I could have done to prevent Eli's death when the Peachey house exploded. The bishop and I barely escaped with our own lives and Ada Mae had also been killed. But the guilt still kept me awake at night. Now both Naomi and Eli were gone—and not so long ago they'd been young lovers, sneaking off to a cornfield for stolen kisses on warm summer nights.

I couldn't speak. John caught my eye and there was sympathy in his expression. He rescued me from the turmoil of my thoughts by speaking up.

"Thank you for your hospitality, Mrs. Yoder. We don't want to keep you from your chores any longer than necessary." He crossed his arms and leaned over the table. "We're investigating a murder that took place in Lancaster County about fifteen years ago. It's been brought to our attention that some of the youth from Blood Rock traveled there in that time period and might know some information about the crime." He lifted his hands. "Now, don't get us wrong. We don't believe these boys committed any crimes. We just want to ask them some questions, see what they might remember about the days leading up to the murder."

John's handling of the question was smooth and I glanced back at Rebecca to gauge her reaction. She chewed her bottom lip, and then looked at me.

She dropped her voice to a whisper. "Do you swear no one from our community is in trouble? My people have endured so much tragedy lately."

My mouth thinned. "I'm sorry, I can't make any promises, but Marshal Ruthers is being truthful. We don't believe an Amish boy committed the crime, we just have some questions that need to be answered." On a long shot, I added, "Do you know anyone by the name of Jerimiah Suggs?"

She shook her head. "No, never heard that name…" she trailed off.

"Do you know this new fellow, Joshua Miller, who's moving into the community?" I asked on a whim.

"Not personally." She held very still. "I've heard he has a sad story and that's why he came here with his family."

I met John's and Toby's wide-eyed looks with my own. So much tragedy happened within Amish communities. Accidents abounded, and matters that usually involved law enforcement were hidden from the outside and settled within their own authority. Most people had no idea how *not* cozy the lives of some Amish really were.

I wondered if Joshua Miller's arrival meant anything or if it was just a coincidence. My personal experience told me there were few coincidences during criminal investigations. Without any leads to the contrary, I dismissed the Amish man for the time being—but I wouldn't forget him. I had a feeling I'd have a chat with him sooner rather than later.

"It's an important case, Rebecca. If you have any information at all that will help, please," I coaxed.

She glanced at John, then at her fingers as they laced together. "I recall hearing something about the murder of a builder in Lancaster County a long time ago. I believe it happened near the Strasburg community." She glanced around the room. "I know two from Blood Rock who spent time there when they were teenagers."

John, Toby and I straightened in our chairs at her words. Rebecca hesitated, her eyes darting back to the basement door.

"We just want to ask them some questions—that's all. Go on," I urged.

She took a breath. "Seth Hershberger was one of them. He ended up marrying a Lancaster girl and never came back."

My heart quickened when I asked, "Who was the other?"

"Lester Lapp."

5

Late afternoon sun shone through the narrow gaps in the barn's wall, making lines that sliced across the floor. The air smelled like hay and sweaty horse. It was a pleasant aroma that took the edge off the nerves I'd had since leaving Rebecca's farm.

Toby stroked the black horse cross tied in the aisle, while we waited for Lester to return from the shed just outside the barn where a loud phone ringing had sounded a moment earlier.

John brought his hand to his mouth. "You know this man well?"

"No, not really, but we're acquainted." My stomach tightened. "His oldest son, David, shot and killed an Amish teenager last fall. The girl's family and the entire community were so secretive, it was a difficult to crack the case." As an afterthought, I added, "The young man was deemed mentally ill and is institutionalized now."

John made a soft grunting nose. "Maybe it runs in the family?"

My lip turned up at the corner. "If that's the case, it was his mother, Esther, he inherited the crazies from, not his dad. Lester's easygoing and friendly. Not the type of person you'd expect to kill somebody, let alone bludgeon him to an almost unrecognizable state."

"I've been surprised before," John said.

Before I could answer, Lester returned, going straight to the horse. He smiled at Toby who began helping him unbuckle the harness, then he turned to me. "What brings you by, Sheriff? I hope nothing is amiss."

The memory of the first time I'd met Lester tugged at me. It had been at the schoolhouse benefit auction. At that time, Daniel and I weren't an item; instead, we pretended to be dating to infiltrate the community. Lester was one of Daniel's oldest friends and the first person to approach the shunned man at the gathering. He'd been genuinely happy to hear that Daniel was settling down with a woman. It was a while before I learned his son had killed Naomi and that his wife had covered up the crime to protect her son. Since then, I'd become friendly with his youngest son, Mervin, and I'd been present when his injured leg was miraculously healed by Jonas Peachy. As I stared back at Lester while he patiently waited for me to answer, it struck me as odd that he'd been connected to both of the Amish cases I'd worked on in Blood Rock since becoming Sheriff.

"This is John Ruthers and Toby Bryant. They're U.S. marshals working a case in Lancaster County."

Lester shook both men's hands and his smile broadened. "I lived in Lancaster for a short time after I married Esther. David was a toddler and Mervin was just a baby." His smile disappeared. "I was reluctant to leave them, but at the time, there wasn't any work in Blood Rock."

"When was this?" John asked.

Lester pulled the yoke over the horse's head and paused. "Hmm. I reckon it was the fall of 2000. I was back here by Christmas. I couldn't stand being parted from my family. By spring, more opportunities opened up here, and I didn't go back."

"Did anyone else from Blood Rock go to Lancaster at that time?" John continued the questioning, while I stood by, my gaze flicking from the horse to Lester.

"Seth Hershberger went with me. He liked it in Pennsylvania and stayed." He grinned. "He met his wife there. Women hate to leave their families. It's usually the men who uproot to pacify them."

John nodded and Toby lifted the rest of the harness off the horse's back.

"You're well acquainted with horses, aren't you?" Lester asked Toby, motioning for him to follow him into the tack room.

"I spent some time on the rodeo circuit out west before I got into law enforcement. It's one of those things that never really gets out of your blood," Toby said from around the corner.

When Lester appeared with a tote full of brushes, he tossed one to Toby and they began rubbing the horse down.

I was impressed with John's patience. I would have continued with the questioning while Lester hung the harness, but John seemed content waiting. I assumed he didn't want to startle Lester with a slew of questions. He was giving the Amish man time to become comfortable with him and Toby,

and even encourage a friendship of sorts to development between the two horsemen. It was classic psychology 101.

"What kind of work did you do in Lancaster?" Toby asked,
not pausing while he kneeled to brush the horse's legs.

His question had been conversational and Lester answered
in the same way.

"Building houses and barns for Englishers. I was part of a
crew of about eight who worked for Buddy Prowes." My heart
jumped, and Lester abruptly stepped back from the horse.
"That's why you're here, isn't it—because of Buddy's death?"

"Murder—Buddy Prowes was brutally murdered," I said.

Lester ignored my rebuke or perhaps he didn't get it. "Did
they ever find out who did it?"

John shook his head. "We hoped you might remember
something about that time period that can help us out." He
pulled a small notebook from his inside coat jacket—the same
kind I carried in my back pocket. "Buddy's body was discovered on November sixth. You said you returned to Blood
Rock by Christmas. There's a gap of time where you wouldn't
have been working for Buddy. Did you find other work in
Lancaster?"

"Sure did. After Buddy died, I hired on with one of the
dairy farms. I found out that milking cows wasn't really my
thing." Lester rubbed his jaw.

"So it was a combination of missing your family, and being out of a job again, that brought you back to Blood Rock?"
Toby asked. He still knelt beside the horse's leg, brushing over
it slowly.

"More that I missed my family. Just the day before Buddy
died, I'd been thinking about coming home." Lester glanced
at me, worry lighting his eyes.

"Did you go by the same name when you worked for Buddy?" John asked.

"Of course, why wouldn't I?"

"In all these years of investigating the crime, we never came across your name—" he glanced at his notes "—or Seth Hershberger, for that matter. Was he employed by Buddy, too?"

"He was, but when I went to the dairy, he apprenticed with a furniture maker."

"What was Buddy like?" John looked up from his notes. "Did you like him?"

Lester took a breath and dropped the brush into the tote. "He was a difficult man. Sometimes, he was jolly, cracking jokes and slapping you on the back, but he had a temper." Lester exhaled and looked between me and John. "When I got the news, I wasn't surprised to hear what happened to him."

John tilted his head. "Do you know anyone who might have wanted to kill him?"

Lester's lips thinned and he dropped his head. He took off his straw hat and wiped his brow. "Sure—there were a lot of people who probably wanted the man dead, but I can't think of anyone who'd actually do something like that."

It would have been too easy for Lester to give us a name to work with, and I was never that lucky.

He unlatched the horse's halter from the lead ropes at each side and led him out of the barn. He stopped and looked back. "This might sound crazy—" he shifted on his feet "—but I always wondered about Buddy's ex-wife."

When Lester had walked far enough away that he was out of hearing range, Toby and John moved in closer.

"That was interesting," Toby commented, chewing on the end of a long blade of straw that he'd picked up from somewhere without me noticing.

"Lester didn't do it," I said.

"I agree." John looked at his notes. "But what he said about Samantha Prowes should be looked into more thoroughly, and then there's Seth Hershberger to interview."

"You boys have your work cut out for you." I swallowed down the bitter taste of disappointment that my involvement in the investigation was over.

"Actually, do you have any personal days at your disposal, Sheriff?" John asked.

I eyed him, my heartrate speeding up. "I could manage a couple, I suppose, and we're going into a weekend." My brow rose. "Why?"

John glanced at Toby, who nodded.

"Have you ever been to Lancaster County, Sheriff Adams? The oldest Amish settlements in the United States are there— an intriguing area for anyone with connections to the Plain people."

"Stop beating around the bush, Marshal. Why do you want me on board? I have no jurisdiction in Pennsylvania."

A small smile twitched on John's lips. "But we do." His face sobered. "The main reason we haven't been able to crack this case is because of our inability to communicate with the Amish successfully. We don't understand them well enough to read them correctly and get them to open up. I'm impressed with your acceptance by these people. You seem to have a knack at gaining their trust, and you have good instincts. Our goal is to solve this case for Jim, and I believe with your help, we might actually succeed."

My heart fluttered and the warm breeze pushed back the few strands of my hair not tied back in a ponytail. The case had roused my curiosity and the fact that there might be some connection to Blood Rock gave me the nudging of a satisfactory reason to do it. Todd and Bobby could handle the department for a couple of days. Nothing was going on in town or the Amish community.

The only thing that kept me from shouting out yes was Daniel.

"I'll do it, but you boys will have to go on ahead without me. I have a loose end I need to tie up here before I leave."

"It's good to have you on board." John patted my back and Toby winked before pressing his hat down further on his head.

The excited butterflies I'd felt in my stomach a moment before disappeared and were replaced with a heavy knot.

What had I gotten myself into this time?

6

Smoke puffed up from the grill and I inhaled the smell of steaks cooking, making my mouth water. The sky was the buttery yellow of dusk. Crickets chirped loudly in the shrubs alongside the deck. Stretching out on the lounge chair, I stared at Daniel's back. My heart pounded harder even though I was trying to relax.

"Did my sister provide any useful information to the marshals?" Daniel's voice cut the tranquility.

I licked my lips. Daniel looked over his shoulder at me, not trying to hide a small frown.

"She gave us two names of men from your community who traveled to Lancaster County during the time of Buddy's murder."

Daniel shut the grill's lid and took the seat across from me. He sat sideways, meeting my gaze. "It's crazy to think someone from Blood Rock went to Pennsylvania and murdered a man." He shook his head. "They're grasping at straws, if you ask me." When I only pursed my lips, not looking away, he added, "Who did Rebecca mention?"

"A guy by the name of Seth Hershberger. Do you know him?"

Daniel nodded. "I do. He's about my age—doesn't live in the community any longer. I don't know where he is."

"Lancaster County. He got married and settled down there," I said.

Daniel grunted and rose. He went back to the grill and using the tongs, deposited the steaks on a platter. I stood and pushed my glass of wine to the side of the patio table, making room for the dinner plates. Daniel scooped garlic mashed potatoes next to my steak. He added some green beans before setting it down in front of me. His smile was forced and I raised my brows.

"Who's the other man?" he asked in a low voice.

Daniel was worried. I could hardly blame him. He'd spent so many years away from the community he'd grown up in, and in just the past eight months, he'd seen some horrible things happen among his people. And I was always the one who brought the news to him.

"Lester Lapp. But you already knew that, didn't you?" I cut the steak, then pushed a piece around with my fork waiting for his reply.

He rubbed his face. "Yep. You got me."

"Why didn't you volunteer the information when I first told you about the case?"

He shrugged and began cutting his own steak. "Lester didn't kill anyone, you and I both know that."

I leaned back, narrowing my eyes. "How would I know that? I've seen the man on several occasions, but that hardly constitutes understanding what he's capable of."

He snorted. "You're a keen observer of people and I've trusted your gut on many occasions since I met you. But if you're implying that Lester might be the killer just because he was in Lancaster County when Buddy Prowes was murdered, your instincts are failing you."

I searched my memories, trying to recall if I'd mentioned the victim's name to Daniel. With a shiver, I realized I hadn't. It was a small town and an even smaller Amish community. Perhaps his sister had phoned him about our discussion. That wouldn't surprise me in the least. It still bothered me that he might be discussing an open investigation with someone.

I blew out a deliberate breath. I needed to stop being so damned paranoid. I'd end up a bitter and lonely woman if I didn't. There had been times when Daniel had challenged my trust in him, but in the end, he'd always been on my side.

"Have you ever been to Lancaster County?" I blurted out.

His brows lifted and then he chuckled. "I used to be Amish, remember. Of course, I've been there—but it's been many years."

His amused look made me feel stupid and I glanced away and back again. "I don't think Lester had anything to do with the murder, but it turns out he *was* working for Buddy at the time of his death. I'd hoped he could shed some light on the murdered man and his other acquaintances at the time."

He ran his hand through his hair. "That was a long time ago. Did Lester have anything interesting to say?"

I took a bite of the potatoes and chewed. Daniel had outdone himself on the dinner. The food was delicious. It occurred to me that I should be the one cooking for him, but I dismissed the thought. He actually enjoyed cooking and his schedule was more flexible. Maybe someday I'd have the time to make him a meal.

"He thinks Samantha Prowes did her ex-husband in."

Daniel coughed and took a sip of his beer. "Wouldn't the authorities have checked out that possibility when the crime occurred? I thought relatives were always the first suspects."

"John says that she was interviewed extensively, but nothing came up to incriminate her."

He tilted his head. "I don't see why the marshals are going to the trouble of opening up an investigation so many years later. Whatever happened to this man ended with him, right? There were never any other murders in the area. It might have been completely personal."

I bit my lip and studied Daniel. What he said was reasonable, but the way he said it bothered me. He was trying too hard to convince me. By now, he knew my personality. Once a mystery was raised, I couldn't let it go until I discovered the truth.

"I think it was very personal, but that doesn't mean it's all right to allow a vicious murderer to walk free. As law enforcement officers, it's our job to make sure justice is served."

"Our job? Unless someone from Blood Rock is implicated, this is marshal business—not yours."

I looked away and took a deep breath. "Actually, it is my business." I met his gaze. "I'm going to help with the case."

"Whoa—in what capacity?" He leaned over the table, his brow furrowing.

"John wants me to accompany them to Lancaster County where some more interviews need to be conducted." I pushed the food around my plate with the fork. "He thinks my experience with the Amish might be helpful."

"When are you leaving?"

"Tomorrow. I'll be back by Monday."

He lowered his voice. "You're just going to blow off the weekend trip we had planned to the lake?"

I set the fork down. "We can go camping any weekend—it's the beginning of summer." Seeing the hurt on his face, I softened my tone. "This case intrigues me, and I'll only be gone a few days. If you want, you can come along."

He ran his hand through his hair and shook his head. "Not if you leave tomorrow. I have to finish Mrs. Pickett's roof. We're in for some stormy weather over the weekend."

"Then it's not a great time to go camping anyway." I arched my brows and half-smiled.

Daniel laughed, throwing his head back. When he looked back, his eyes widened and he jumped up. "I'll be right back."

He disappeared through his kitchen door, leaving me alone. I pushed the plate away, losing my appetite. I didn't like always putting the job first, but it was a habit I didn't think I could break easily. My sister, Laura, said I was too independent, and she was probably right.

When Daniel reappeared, he was walking more leisurely with a lopsided grin and an excited look. Butterflies exploded inside my stomach and my groin tingled. He had that effect on my body, and most of the time I hated it, but at the moment, since we had the rest of the evening ahead of us, I welcomed the sweet sensations.

"I was going to do this over the weekend—planned it out perfectly, but with you, I can't schedule anything. So I guess I'm going to have to make do with the little time we have together."

My heart began pounding and I opened my mouth, but he held out his finger, silencing me.

"For once, Serenity, let me do the talking."

I slumped back in the chair, lifted my chin and waited. The sky darkened to a dull gray and the air cooled, sending goosebumps along my arms. I ignored the change in temperature.

Daniel kneeled in front of me, swallowed and then cleared his throat. My heartbeat banged in my ears.

"You're probably going to think I'm rushing things, but I don't care." He pulled something from his pocket, folding his hand over it. "I need to make you mine—for eternity—and I don't want to wait any longer."

My eyes bulged when he opened his hand. *It was a ring.* A silver band, sprinkled with small diamonds that sparkled. The large rock in the middle made my jaw drop. Even in the dusky lighting, it twinkled with a brightness of its own.

I could hardly breathe and the hammering in my chest was almost painful.

"Will you take me as your husband, Serenity—will you marry me?"

I couldn't quite catch my breath. I blinked many times, and tears leaked from my eyes. "You want to get married?" I choked out. "For real?"

He grunted, grasped my hand and pressed the ring into my palm. "I tell you every day I love you. Is it so hard to believe I want to marry you?" He searched my stunned eyes and his smile disappeared. "Dammit, why do you have to be so difficult about everything? It's a simple yes or no answer." He moved closer. "Either you love me and want to make it official—or you don't."

For all the chaos of emotions I was experiencing, his demanding tone made me bristle. "I think it's a little more complicated than that. This is a serious matter—one we shouldn't take lightly or jump into too soon."

Daniel stood up and turned away. "So you're declining my offer. It doesn't surprise me." He hung his head, shaking it. "I feared your feelings weren't the same as mine. I get it—your job is your world and there isn't much room for anything or *anyone* else."

I rose, reached out and touched his shoulder. He flinched away, but didn't leave.

I inhaled, struck by the throbbing in my chest. With steady determination, I cleared my mind and allowed memories of my time with Daniel to wash over me. Ever since the first moment I'd laid eyes on him, when he'd put a new roof on my house, I'd had a crush on him. But now, it wasn't his rugged handsomeness that made my stomach do somersaults. It was the all-consuming way he kissed me, the way he touched me, the way he followed me into dangerous situations unconditionally—the way he loved me. No man had ever loved me so deeply. Even though the intensity of his feelings terrified me sometimes, the fact that he was willing to leave his bachelor days behind him for good and make me his wife filled me with something I hadn't felt in a long time—hopefulness.

"You didn't give me a chance to answer," I said quietly.

He whirled around. His face was still as stone, but his eyes had brightened.

I made a snapping noise. "I'm sorry I messed the whole thing up—I was surprised. I thought you'd be pissed at me for going out of town this weekend. A marriage proposal was the last thing I was expecting."

"Well?" He held out his hand, unfurling his fingers.

The ring was small in his large, calloused palm, but it glistened with the energy of his love. More tears spilled from my eyes and I wiped them away with the back of my hand.

My breath shuddered out of my chest. "Yes, Daniel. I'll marry you."

He slid the ring onto my finger in a quick motion, like he was afraid I'd change my mind if he took too long. It fit perfectly and I stared down at it with wide eyes. "It's beautiful," I managed to say before his arms encircled me.

It was a bone-crushing hug and Daniel's own tears dampened my neck as he buried his face there. Normally, a guy crying would have freaked me out, but this time, I was all right with it.

When he finally loosened his hold and leaned back, he was smiling.

I didn't want to ruin the moment, but I couldn't keep quiet any longer. "I hope you're okay with a long engagement?"

He laughed. "I want to do it next week."

My mouth dropped open and I felt the blood drain from my face. "Seriously?"

He swooped down and picked me up. Before I could protest, he nuzzled my cheek. "Darling, you can have as long an engagement as you want—as long as you keep that ring on your finger—and move in with me."

I was able to breathe normally again and I grinned. "I can agree to that."

His mouth came down on mine and his tongue slipped between my lips. In a display of impressive coordination, he carried me into the house and closed the door behind us without interrupting the kiss.

When he dropped me onto the bed and crawled on top of me, I really regretted agreeing to help the marshals out with the Buddy Prowes' investigation.

The last thing I wanted to do was leave Daniel now.

7

I slunk along behind the marshals, barely paying attention to the activity around us. The afternoon was cloudy and thick with humidity. The darkening sky threatened rain, and I hoped a passing shower would cool things down.

Pulling an elastic band from my jean pocket, I finger combed my blonde hair into a ponytail. Since I wasn't the sheriff in this town, I was comfortable in jeans and a button up, casual blouse. But my 9 mm Glock was securely attached to my calf. I never went anywhere without it.

Toby had shed his jacket in the car. He wore the same cowboy hat and boots, and carried his sidearm visible at his hip like a gunslinger. It worked with his swaggering walk that would have fit perfectly in the Wild West.

I was impressed that John still had on his suit jacket, although he'd lost the tie. I knew his weapon was holstered across his chest. He slowed his purposeful stride. "How are we going to find our man in this crowd?"

"Trust me, they all know each other. We'll find him," I said.

Toby eyed me with the same incredulous look. On both sides of us, vendors were lined up in the grass along a gravel roadway that led up into a giant white barn. Some English people were sprinkled among the tables, but mostly Amish men, women and children were selling everything from jars of honey and jams to furniture and hand tools. There were also animals—tons of animals. Pigs were crowded into crates, and ponies and miniature goats were tied to the back of buggies with homemade wooden signs advertising their prices.

I paused in front of a row of cages stacked high. Rabbits looked out with twitching noses and chickens flapped their wings. I never knew so many different kinds of each existed. And then there were the puppies—fat, cuddly, adorable puppies everywhere. John had to urge Toby and me onward twice after we couldn't resist stopping to *ooh* and *ah* over infant cocker spaniels and labradoodles.

"The Amish are notorious for their puppy mills." John wrinkled his nose at a box full of hound puppies.

"Don't you like dogs?" I asked him.

His eyes flashed. "I love 'em. That's why it bothers me to see so many here today. They can't possibly all be sold to good homes. Most will end up in shelters or worse yet, at the bottom of a pond."

I grabbed his arm, tugging him to a stop. "Are you serious?"

He shook his head. "Wish I wasn't. My mother is a huge animal activist. She volunteers at our local shelter and knows all about these mass breeders." He broke into a smile. "Believe me, if Mom was here, she'd be giving these people a hard time."

"I like your mother already." I lifted my brows.

Toby leaned over. "She makes a mean chicken-n-dumplings, too."

John blushed. "Maybe you'll get to meet her someday, Sheriff. She does love to cook."

"I'll plan on it, after we get our man."

"I really like a woman who knows what she wants." Toby winked at me, and then I was the one blushing.

I wasn't deceived by his boyish charm. Underneath the wide grin and twinkling blue eyes, he was a sharp shooter—the type who never missed, and never regretted his shots.

"Leave her alone. She's engaged," John scolded.

"Only recently." Toby snickered.

My stomach clenched and I cleared my throat. "How did you know that?"

Toby motioned to my hand. "You weren't wearing any bling yesterday, but today there's a giant rock on your finger." His smile turned into a smirk. "Was Daniel a little jealous about you taking a trip out of state with us this weekend?"

My face heated to an uncomfortable degree and I glared back at Toby. He reminded me a lot of Todd, having the same inappropriate flirty personality in the workplace. But I'd been plagued by my first deputy since middle school, and he could get away with the teasing. This cowboy was acting too familiar for the short time I'd known him, but I *was* impressed by his observation skills. If he wasn't so annoying, I'd want him working for me in Blood Rock.

I took a step into his personal space and he held his ground, although he leaned back slightly. I pointed my finger into his chest. "My personal life is none of your business."

John interrupted before Toby could respond with more than a feigned look of surprise that asked *Why are you picking on me?*

"Now that you two got that out of your systems, let's find this guy," John said.

Toby fanned out his arm, directing me to take the lead. I passed by without looking back.

A white-bearded Amish man with a cage full of doves caught my eye. No one was with him and he looked bored, staring at the throng of people passing by his table.

"Excuse me, the birds are lovely. How much are they?" I pressed my finger against the cage to touch a white feather sticking out.

"Twenty-five dollars for a single and forty for a pair," he replied.

His English was forced and I realized he was one of the Amish who didn't talk to outsiders much.

I nodded and as smoothly as I could transition the conversation, I asked, "When we stopped by Seth Hershberger's house, his son told us his father would be here selling Australian shepherds. Do you know where he's set up?"

The old man pointed. "He has them at his buggy, around back, behind the barn." He covered the side of his mouth as if telling a secret. "He doesn't have to pay the vendor fee that way."

I nodded and forced a smile. "Thank you."

We took the most direct path, straight through the barn, squeezing through the crowd, not pausing to look at any more animals. Although I did slow a little at the pen with the baby pigs. They were black and white, and one of them was squealing. It was an awful sound and I wanted to make sure the little beast wasn't being hurt.

We stepped through the doors on the other side of the barn just as it began to sprinkle. The drizzle only made the air feel thicker.

I spotted a man with a long brown beard leaning against a crate in between a buggy and wagon. I jutted my chin towards the man, and John and Toby followed my gaze.

The speckled puppies squirmed in the crate when I peeked in. A fluffy brown and white one jumped up, whining at me. I couldn't resist reaching in to stroke its head.

"Here—you should hold her. She's lonely, misses her mama," the man said.

He plucked the pup up and thrust her into my hands before I could object. She wiggled until I pressed her warm body against my chest. The wonderful smell of puppy breath filled my nose. It had been a long time since I'd held a puppy, and the weight of it in my arms felt nice.

Toby knelt beside the crate, petting the others in turn, but John was all business. "Are you Seth Hershberger?"

The man's gaze shot in John's direction, but he recovered quickly. He thrust his hand out to shake John's. "Why yes, I am." He paused. "Have we met?"

"I'm Marshal John Ruthers and this is my partner, Toby Bryant." He nodded at me. "Serenity is a consultant on a case we're working on."

Seth features tightened, but he retained a pleasant tone. "Am I in some kind of trouble?"

I thought it was an odd question coming from an Amish man. I half expected him to make a run for it, and the last thing I wanted to do was drop the puppy to chase the lanky man through the crowd.

"No, no. We just want to ask you a few questions, if that's all right?" John asked.

"Of course. What's it about?"

"Bobby Prowes." John paused. If I had to guess, I'd say he was waiting for the impact of the name to settle over Seth.

Seth's face widened in recognition. "I haven't heard that name in forever."

"So you know the man?" John asked.

"Sure, I worked for him when I was—" he lifted his eyes, as if searching his memory "—about eighteen. He had a building crew—young men mostly—both English and Amish."

I hugged the puppy closer, shielding her the best I could from the light rain. I relaxed, blowing out a quiet breath. I was glad this Amish man was being open about his involvement with Buddy. He certainly didn't seem to have anything horrible to hide.

He took off his hat, wiped his brow and replaced it. "For a minute there, I thought you were one of those animal rights people." Seeing my eyes narrow, he hurriedly added, "I thought it would be nice for my kids to raise a batch of puppies off our cattle dog. This is my first time selling any."

John ignored what Seth had said. "Were you working for Buddy at the time of his murder?"

Seth nodded. "We were in the middle of a job when it happened. Another builder came in and finished the job. I went to work for Homestead Furniture and learned the trade. I never went back to building houses."

"How long did you know Buddy?"

"Not very long—maybe two months. I'm from Blood Rock, Indiana, originally. I came up here for work, met a girl and the rest is history." Seth grinned and I found myself liking him.

The rain picked up, and Seth reached over and took my puppy to place her back in the crate. Toby helped Seth lift the crate into the wagon and together, they pulled a canvas tarp over it. The warm place against my chest where the pup had rested quickly turned cold.

"Was Buddy a good guy to work for?" I asked.

Seth turned around slowly. He seemed reluctant to answer. "I wish I could say that he was, but I can't. He threw a board at me one time when I didn't hear him giving orders." He pointed to his ear. "I have to wear hearing aids. It was an honest mistake, but Buddy got really angry with me."

I digested the information, beginning to dislike Buddy. It was no wonder someone did him in, although it was never easy working a case where the victim was an asshole.

"Do you remember him having altercations with anyone else on the crew?" John asked.

Seth's mouth thinned and he drew in a steady breath. "He yelled at everyone at some point or another. He was big guy, so no one argued with him. But..." He stopped and looked between the three of us, then lowered his voice. "There was one time he got into a fight with his wife...or maybe they were divorced, I can't remember. Anyway, she stopped by and they began shouting at each other. I think it was something about how she didn't like him parking his car in front of her house— she accused him of spying on her." He smoothed down his beard with his hand. "She slapped him across the face, then he shoved her hard, and she fell to the ground. My friend, Lester, and I wanted to go over and help her up, but we were afraid to. Everyone stopped working and stared."

"Did someone call the police?" I asked.

"No. The woman jumped up, yelled some more and got into her car and drove away." He shook his head. "It was as if she was used to that sort of thing happening."

"Who do you think murdered Buddy?" John took a step closer to Seth, leaning over in a *Hey, aren't we friends?* sort of way.

Seth's eyes became distant as he stared at the barn, and the people flooding back outside now that the sky had brightened and the rain had stopped. "I wouldn't hazard a guess. It could have been anyone."

I glanced at John. His mouth thinned into a grim line. "Thank you for talking to us, Seth. Can we have your phone number, just in case we need to follow up on a question?"

Seth reached into his back pocket. He pulled out a plain white business card and handed it to John. "That's for the furniture shop. I'm there all week and sometimes on Saturdays. There's no phone at our house, so that's the best way to reach me."

"How much are the puppies?" Toby asked, shooting me a sideways glance. I wanted to smack the teasing look off his face.

Seth straightened. "Seventy-five each. They're not papered, but I wormed 'em and did their first shots."

Silence hung in the air as the three men stared at me. I heard a yip and a whine, but said nothing.

When we got back into John's car, I took shotgun and Toby climbed into the backseat.

"I thought you fell in love with that pup," Toby said.

"I don't have time for a dog in my life—I can barely keep up with Daniel." I buckled the seat belt and turned to John. "I think we need to talk to Samantha Prowes."

"My thoughts exactly," John replied.

8

The house was small, white and neat as a button. Trimmed shrubbery lined the walkway and a slick-coated black cat was curled up on one of the flowery padded chairs on the porch. Bright pink petunias draped from hanging baskets and the sunshine beating down on the wet grass created a thick, greenhouse feeling.

I wiggled, pulling my damp shirt away from my chest and flapping it. "If this weather is any indication, it's going to be a scorching summer," I commented.

John wasn't even sweating, and I wondered how he managed it, still wearing the dark coat. Toby had rolled up his sleeves, but wasn't reacting to the heat the way I was.

"We're going to have to tread lightly with Buddy's ex-wife. Jim interviewed her extensively, but it's been a while. Sometimes, people recall bits of information years later that are useful," John said.

"Yeah, and sometimes they create new realities of the event. It can go either way," I countered.

"True, but if this woman was involved in the murder in any way, enough time has passed that she might just let something slip." John nodded for Toby to knock on the door.

A boy, about ten years old, peeked through the narrow opening. Blond hair hung down over his eye and he shook his head to clear his vision.

"Is your mom home?" John asked.

"Mom!" The boy shouted, then he ran back into the house.

"Kids," John muttered, rubbing his ear.

The woman who stepped up to the door was as blonde as her son. She was shorter than me and petite. She wore just enough makeup to enhance her attractive features without overdoing it, and in khaki pants and a green blouse, she was nicely dressed.

I swallowed down my surprise. Samantha Prowes didn't match the picture I'd already created in my head.

"Can I help you?" she said in a soft voice, adding to my disbelief that she was capable of murder and bludgeoning a corpse.

John introduced us and Samantha invited us in. She offered us tea and coffee, which we politely refused, and asked her son to play outside.

Once we were seated, and before John had the opportunity to say anything, she spoke up. "This is about Buddy, isn't it?"

John reacted smoothly. "Why do you assume that?"

A smile tugged at her lips and she flipped her shoulder-length hair back. I guessed she was about five years older than me, but had that innocent, damsel-in-distress look that made her appear younger.

"I have a law degree and work at a small firm in town." She paused, as though she were savoring our surprised expressions, and then she went on, "Your shocked looks are nothing new—I guess it's my appearance." She shrugged. "After Buddy was killed in the woods behind the house, a lot of unwarranted suspicion fell on me. Everyone was whispering behind my back. It nearly ruined my life. After about a year, I got fed up with it and enrolled in evening law classes while I continued to work full time at the bank. I earned my degree five years later and ever since, I've been focused on women's rights, and protecting those unable to defend themselves against the same kind of assumptions I dealt with."

I sighed softly, feeling deflated. The fact that she was a lawyer pretty much shot to hell any chance of her slipping up and incriminating herself or an accomplice.

John must have felt the same way I did because he slumped in his chair. "Recently, a woman came forward to the original marshal on the case, Jim Allen. He passed away shortly afterwards, but forwarded the file on to me."

"Tonya Sanders, right?" Samantha said. When John nodded, she added, "She always thought one of the Amish boys on the building crew killed him."

"What do *you* think about her assertion?" John asked.

Toby and I turned back to Samantha. I was impressed with how John changed the course of the conversation so fluidly after the revelation that Buddy's ex-wife, and prime suspect, was now a lawyer and already knew all about the new allegations.

"A lot of people hated Buddy, including me. I find it hard to believe one of those mild-mannered, quiet young men would have done such a thing. I mean, shooting a man is very different from pounding his head in with the blunt end of an ax." She said the words with the cool aloofness of an anchorwoman reciting a murder on the evening news. A chill ran up my spine as she stood and walked over to a chest of small drawers in the corner of the room. "I always wondered about *this*. I know you guys have a picture of it in your file." She pulled out an envelope and handed it to John. "But nothing ever came of it."

John opened the envelope and pulled a folded piece of paper from it. He glanced at it and handed it to me.

The words were foreign and scribbled messily on the paper, but I forced them out anyway. "*Gott segen eich.* What does that mean?"

"I don't know. I assumed it was Pennsylvania Dutch and I asked some of the local Amish, but no one would give me a straight answer. They're pretty tight lipped around here, only talking to outsiders when business is involved. They seem to have their own authority system and don't like outsiders butting into what they assume are internal affairs." She shook her head.

I snorted and pulled my cellphone from my pocket. "Do you mind if I take a picture? I have someone who will translate this."

"Go ahead." She waved her hand.

"Where was this note left originally?" John asked.

"In the driver seat of Buddy's car. The authorities took photographs, but they completely dismissed the note. I was allowed to gather up his personal belongings—" she shrugged "—and kept the note." She caught the rise of my brows. "I was the only other kin he had besides his brother, Brent, and he wasn't interested in the little things."

I sent the picture and looked up, waiting. "Does Brent live around here?"

"Just a little ways north on Hinton Road. He took over Buddy's contracting company after the murder, but he wasn't able to keep it going."

"Why, what happened?" I glanced at my phone, but there weren't any new messages.

"With Buddy gone, Isaiah Coblenz expanded his own building business. He provided better work for less money than Brent could pull off."

"Was he a business threat when Buddy owned it?" I asked, feeling that this part of the story was significant.

Her brow shot up and she chuckled. "I'm sorry. I forgot you didn't know Buddy. No one dared to outbid him on a job." Her lips pinched together in a tight smile. "He was one of those guys no one wanted to mess with, if you know what I mean."

I met her gaze. "Yeah, I know the type." I took a breath, processing the information.

Even though I felt compelled to pull my notebook from my back pocket, I didn't. John was already scribbling notes on his. Toby sat quietly to the side, his hat on his lap, and his eyes darting everywhere. I had to admit, I sometimes forgot he was even there, but I sure did appreciate his alertness.

My gut told me that Samantha wasn't being entirely honest with us. She said all the right things in just the right way. It was as though she'd prepared for this moment for a long time. Jim Allen probably came up against the same wall, even though the woman wasn't a lawyer at the time.

"So the Amish were too intimidated by Buddy to run their businesses properly, but they didn't have such qualms with the brother?" I said.

"That's right. Oh, and by the way, Tonya Sanders is Brent's long-time girlfriend. They've been an item for over twenty years and have three kids together."

Her words rippled through my mind just as my phone vibrated in my hands. I looked down.

Daniel gave me the translation, followed by a kissy-faced emoji.

I glanced between John and Samantha. "God bless you—that's what those words mean."

Samantha made a humming noise and gazed out the window, while John wrote it down.

I rubbed my forehead. *This isn't a good sign at all.*

9

"**M**aybe the note didn't have anything at all to do with the murder," Toby suggested.

I took a bite of the noodle-mashed potato concoction and stared at the colorful quilt hanging on the wall in the Amish restaurant. I savored the taste in my mouth as I thought about the handwritten note.

When I swallowed, I looked between John and Toby. John was enjoying a meatloaf and sweet potato dinner while looking through Buddy's file. Toby had ordered the same entree as me and was focused on eating it.

"It was on Buddy's seat and it wasn't crumpled like it would be if someone had sat on it. I think whoever killed Buddy left the note there for a reason," I said.

John glanced up, meeting my gaze over his reading glasses. "For what purpose, Sheriff?"

I took a sip of my cola. The restaurant was filled mostly with Amish families. A young girl in a lavender dress stared openly at me and I forced myself to smile back and then looked away. Here, we were the oddity.

"Either the note was literal and the person who committed the crime was making a final statement to Buddy or, what I think is more likely, it was a diversion to direct authorities away from the true killer," I said.

John smiled. "Well done. I think your latter assumption is correct, but why point the finger at the Amish when they're pacifist people?" He lifted a few papers from the file and waved them in the air. "Jim didn't get anywhere when he tried to investigate them."

I studied the map of Lancaster County spread out on the table. "We're here, in Strasburg, the main tourist hub of the Amish, but see? Samantha's house is closer to Womelsdorf, a completely different community."

"Aren't they all connected?" John scrunched his brows.

I snorted. "That's what I used to think, but I know better now." I traced the map with my finger. "There are thousands of Plain people living in this area, but they're split up into separate church groups. Each group contains between fifteen and twenty-five families. When a church grows too large to accommodate services at family farms, they split up, forming new churches."

"How does this affect the investigation?" Toby spoke up.

"If Jim was talking to people in Strasburg or New Holland, he wasn't reaching the Amish who were associated with Buddy. News and gossip spread from church to church, but an Amish family here—" I pointed to a random spot on the map, then slid my finger to another spot "—might have little connection to a family here." I leaned back. "We need to talk to the Amish in Womelsdorf."

"I want to interview Brent Prowes, too," John said.

"Of course, but his girlfriend, Tonya Sanders, might be the better choice to begin with," I said.

John nodded and began eating his dinner in earnest when my phone vibrated on the table.

"Hey, Todd, what do you have for me?" I answered.

"I ran Brent Prowes and Tonya Sanders' names. They're both clean to the point of boring. Only a few speeding tickets came up between the two of them."

"Okay, thanks. How's Blood Rock fairing?"

"Fairly quiet here. Tony Manning stopped by this morning—said he wanted to have a talk with you. I told him you were out of town and he made a rude comment about your work ethics." Todd grunted.

I rolled my eyes and rubbed my forehead. As if the unique aspects to this criminal investigation weren't enough, I'd have to deal with Tony when I returned home.

"I hope you reminded him I'm entitled to personal days. He sure took enough of them when he had the job."

"Yeah, I got into it with him, and so did Bobby. It was like he showed up just to ruin our day." Todd cleared his throat. "I sure hope you're heading home soon. I don't get paid enough to deal with that man's shit."

I sighed. "I'll take care of it on Monday."

"I managed to pull a picture of Tonya up from an article that ran a year ago in the local newspaper out there. She works at a restaurant called Yoder's Smorgasbord. Thought it might be useful—I'm sending it now. Be safe, boss," Todd said, and then hung up.

I put my phone down. "What's this place called?"

"Yoder's Smorgasbord, I think," Toby replied.

Small world.

"Brent and his girlfriend have no previous criminal activity, but supposedly, she used to work here." I scooped up some more of the delicious potatoes on my fork. "Hard to believe someone who could commit such a brutal crime would go the next fifteen years without acting out again."

"Buddy's murderer had a motive and felt justified in his actions. It's possible that it was a one-time deal," John said.

I met his gaze. "If someone has the propensity to do that to another person, especially someone they know, they're capable of doing it again."

My phone vibrated against the table and I pulled up the new message with the picture Todd had sent. I looked around and searched the restaurant. Many of the servers were young Amish women, but a few were Englishers. I spotted a woman with curly brown hair and glanced back at the photo Todd had sent.

"Interviewing Tonya isn't going to be too difficult." I lifted my phone for them to see and then jutted my chin out. They turned in their seats, following the direction of my chin. "The woman over there is Tonya."

"Well, damn," Toby said.

John tilted his head. "I echo your sentiments entirely."

I motioned our server over. Her hair was neatly pinned beneath her cap and the apron she wore over her hunter green dress was pristine white. I wondered about her life. Was she courting a boy she was in love with or was she already married? Since the Amish didn't wear wedding rings, it was impossible to tell. At least the men began growing their beards when they were hitched, giving an indication of their marital status.

"Are you ready for your check?" she asked.

"That'll be fine." I leaned forward. "Is that Tonya Sanders over there?"

She followed my gaze. "Why yes. Would you like to speak with her? I can get her for you."

"That would be perfect. Thank you."

I pushed my plate aside and watched as our server spoke to Tonya, then pointed at our table. Tonya nodded and hurried over.

When she reached us, I stood and extended my hand. It occurred to me after the fact that I was stepping on John's toes by taking the lead with Tonya, but dismissed the thought. It was Todd's information that gave us the heads up that the woman was in the same room as us.

"I'm Serenity Adams and this is John Ruthers and Toby Bryant. We're law enforcement. Do you have a minute to speak with us?"

Tonya looked to be in her mid-thirties. She had a blemish-free, round face and the lines at the edges of her green eyes indicated she laughed a lot.

She wiped her hands on her apron. "It's the end of my shift and I just signed out, so sure—" she shrugged "—I guess so."

I pulled out the chair beside me and she took it. I looked at John and he got the hint.

"Do you remember Buddy Prowes?" John asked.

"Of course. He was killed out behind Samantha's house. Who could forget something like that?"

"Did you know him well?" I asked.

She crossed her arms on the table. "I wasn't sleeping with him if that's what you're asking."

I hid a smile at John's red face. "No, no, that's not what I meant," I stammered.

"I *was* sleeping with his brother, Brent, and have been until recently. That's how I knew Buddy." She dropped her voice. "He wasn't a very nice man—I didn't spend any more time with him than was necessary, if you know what I mean." She nudged me with her elbow and I nodded understanding.

"Recently?" I raised my brows. "Aren't you and Brent still together?"

"Naw. That's the beauty of not tying the knot—you can up and leave whenever you want." Her words swirled around in my mind and I thought of Daniel. I'd been too preoccupied with the case to think about him much lately, but a shiver passed through me.

I glanced at John and he tilted his head, encouraging me to continue. I took a breath. "I've been asking myself the same thing about *tying the knot*." I flashed my ring for her to see. "If you don't mind me asking, why did you call it quits?"

Her lips pinched and she made a clucking noise. "We've been together nearly eighteen years, have kids, a house and everything, but his heart has always been with another." She shot me a warning look. "Men don't forget their first love. The best thing is if they get to experience some time with that woman, get to know her faults, and they fall out of love naturally. When they never have the chance, there's always that question rattling around in their mind—*what if*—even though they have a good woman right beside them, who loves them more than the other one ever would have."

My chest clenched when I saw the hurt in Tonya's eyes, but her story made me think about David Lapp and his obsession with Naomi Beiler. That obsession had ended with Naomi's murder.

I took a chance and pressed further. "Was it an Amish girl?"

Tonya's eyes widened, but she didn't hesitate to answer. "She's not a girl anymore—she's a woman my age." She glanced over her shoulder. The restaurant was noisy with conversation and the clinking of dishes. After a quick look around, she turned back. "All these years she never married, teasing Brent with the possibility she'd leave the Amish and go English." Her lip turned up at the corner. "Well, she never left and she's finally tying the knot next week."

My brow furrowed. "Isn't that a good thing for you and Brent?"

"You'd think, but ever since he found out about the wedding, he's been a different person. I decided it's better to move on. I just couldn't take being second fiddle to a daydream anymore."

I offered a small smile. "Thank you for being honest with us."

"If you need anything else, I'm working day shift all weekend," she said, smiling at each of us and standing abruptly.

When she was gone, Toby found his voice. "I don't see how any of this fits together."

"Motive," John answered and met my gaze. "I'd like to talk to this mystery Amish woman, but there's probably no hope in that, is there?"

Our server appeared with the check and handed it to John.

Before she turned to leave, I reached out and lightly touched her arm. She looked back at me expectantly and I said, "Tonya mentioned the big wedding next week. It must be a relief to her family that she's finally found the right one after all these years?" I asked, feigning friendship with a woman I'd just learned about.

"Oh, yes, it's all the talk in the community." She was bubbly with enthusiasm. "I can't imagine being single until thirty-four years old—Miriam is so old, but the Coblenzes are known for marrying later, just not *that* late." She took a breath. "Will you be at the wedding? I heard a lot of out-of-towners are coming for it."

I nodded, spreading my lips. "Yes, hopefully we are—as long as business doesn't call us away. It's on…" I trailed off, pretending to search my memory.

"Thursday morning." She grinned. "I understand. It's odd to Englishers that we usually have our weddings on Thursday mornings. It's custom. The service begins at nine o'clock, but since it lasts nearly three hours, we don't expect our English friends to sit so long. Most of the time, the outsiders arrive at the end of the service and they attend the dinner afterwards."

A stern-faced woman poked her head out of the kitchen and called out to our server in Pennsylvania Dutch.

"I have to go. I hope to see you at the wedding."

I stopped her again. "What's your name?"

"Louise Schwartz." She smiled and hustled away.

"Very smooth," Toby said.

I looked away. Louise seemed like a nice girl and I hated playing her. "I've learned that young Amish women love to gossip. Their loose lips have helped me on more than one occasion."

"That's why we brought you along, Sheriff." John's firm nod lifted my spirits a little bit.

But I knew that prying into Amish lives was a murky business, and usually in the end, I discovered very unpleasant things.

10

Morning dew was heavy in the grass and a thin mist rose above the fields we passed by as we bounced up Isaiah Coblenz's gravel driveway. Cows munched beside the fence and a rooster crowed. It was such a peaceful setting, and yet here we were, investigating a cold case murder.

"Seth Hershberger works for Isaiah Coblenz. Brent Prowes had a crush on Isaiah's daughter—that's our connection," John said.

"I agree, it's intriguing." The breeze blowing into the car was warm and damp, and I rolled the window down further. The sun was beginning to shine through gaps in the clouds, promising another scorching day.The furniture shop came into view. A wooden sign hung below the eaves of a barnlike structure. A buggy was parked in front of the entrance. The black horse tied to the hitching rail was pawing at the ground. John began to turn into the space beside the buggy, but I waved him on.

"Let's go to the house first. Amish men are usually more tightlipped than the women. I'd like to catch Miriam off guard."

John straightened the car and proceeded up the driveway until we reached the white farmhouse on the hill. Clothes were already hung on the line to dry and several women were bent over in the vegetable garden next to the house.

John put the car in park and shut off the engine. When he reached for the door handle, I stopped him. "I think it might be better if I talked to her alone. A couple of strange men might intimidate her."

John frowned and stared at me. "All right. You have ten minutes. See what you can come up with."

I rolled my eyes at his proposed time constraint. I'd seen how uncomfortable he'd been around Rebecca, her daughter and the servers at the restaurant. Amish women put him on edge as much as the men bothered me. I glanced at Toby. Nothing seemed to ruffle his feathers. At the moment, he was immersed in reading a book about the Amish he'd picked up in the lobby of our hotel. He didn't even bother to glance at me as I exited the vehicle.

A woman with mostly gray hair poking out from beneath her cap straightened up and stared at me. Her burgundy dress flapped around her in the stiff breeze.

"*Hullo!* The shop is down below." She pointed at the building we'd just passed.

"I didn't come for furniture. I want to talk to Miriam. Is she available?" I held my breath.

The woman called over her shoulder in Pennsylvania Dutch and a younger woman looked up. She dropped her digging tool and wiped her hands on the sides of her blue dress.

Her hair was the same shade of blonde as mine and several strands stuck out from beneath her cap. Her bright blue eyes were full of curiosity when she approached me.

"I'm Miriam—may I help you?"

I glanced at the older woman. She squinted at me and placed her hands on her hips.

"Can we talk in private?" I met the hard gaze from the woman, who I guessed was Miriam's mother from the similarity of their features. There was a long, uncomfortable pause before she blew out a full breath.

"I suppose so." She turned and said a few words to Miriam before returning to work.

Miriam directed me toward the house, up the front porch steps and into a rocking chair. She pulled another rocker closer to me. Before she sat down, she tilted her head. "Are you thirsty? I made lemonade this morning."

I gazed out at the farm below us. The sun had burned off the mist and the grass sparkled in the light. A few chickens pecked in front of the porch and I heard the squeals of children playing in the back yard. Only on investigations when I questioned Amish women was I offered food and drink. That never happened in the outside world.

"No, thank you." I smiled.

Miriam fidgeted with her fingers in her lap. Freckles spread over her nose, making her appear younger than I knew she was. The slight lines around her eyes and her slender face gave her away. She was attractive, but not any more so than Tonya was. Men were fickle sometimes. Or possibly it was just the idea of wanting what they couldn't have.

"Do you know Brent Prowes?" I ventured.

Her eyes widened and her mouth dropped opened. The expression only lasted an instant before she composed herself, forcing her face back to neutral. "I know of him. He's one of the Amish drivers."

My brow furrowed. "I thought he was a builder."

"He used to do that. But now he's a handyman, doing odd jobs and he drives our people." The color drained from her cheeks even though she offered me a polite smile. I felt a pang of sympathy for her.

The last thing I wanted to do was cause Miriam undo trouble by having her mother or one of the other women overhearing our conversation, so I leaned forward and dropped my voice. "I was told you two know each other quite well." When she began to speak, I raised my hand. "I'm not here to judge. I'm the sheriff from the Blood Rock Amish community in Indiana. I'm working the Buddy Prowes' murder case with federal marshals."

She looked around. When her eyes returned to me, she said slowly, "That was so long ago."

"New information came to light and the case has been reopened. No one wants such a brutal crime to go unsolved."

"I don't know how I can help." Miriam glanced back at the garden. Her mother and the other women were still working, paying no attention to us.

"We're trying to paint a picture of what was going on around the time of his murder." I drew in a quick breath. "It came to our attention that Brent Prowes is infatuated with you. Is that true?"

Miriam's face turned pink, and she shushed me with an urgent finger to her mouth. "It's something we don't talk about." She grimaced. "He's a kind man. I befriended him after his brother's death. He seemed so lost." She hurriedly added, "But our relationship was never a romantic one."

"How did you even meet him?" I asked, knowing how rare it was for Amish women to interact alone with English men.

"He drove our people back then, too. There were times when he'd take me to town and we'd talk. He was always around our events, so I saw him often."

"Did you have any idea he was sweet on you?"

She looked away, took a breath and then met my gaze. "He told me. I felt terrible for him. I would never leave my people. We were from different worlds—it wouldn't have worked out."

"But you never married anyone else all these years," I pointed out.

She tilted her head. "I can't say it was because of Brent. I didn't find a suitor I felt right about until recently." She grinned and covered her mouth with her hand. "My wedding to Joseph Mast is next week."

The sound of the creaking of our rocking chairs was relaxing. Daniel popped into my mind and I worked to stop myself from grinning.

"When is your wedding ceremony?" Miriam blurted out.

My heart raced. "What makes you ask that?"

"Your ring is beautiful. I know something of your customs." She sat back, looking pleased with herself "On that particular finger, it means you're spoken for."

I exhaled. "He just popped the question a few days ago. It's all kind of new to me." I looked down at the ring and twirled it with my thumb. "I usually forget all about the ring—until someone reminds me of it or it catches my eye."

"In my people's eyes, I'm an oddity for marrying so late in life. But for you, it's rather expected, isn't it?"

I chuckled. "I don't consider us to be old women. Life is a journey. Sometimes we get to the same place at different times."

"Well said." Miriam crossed her hands in her lap. "Are you sure you don't want some of that lemonade?"

I caught John staring at us from inside the car and his impatient frown dragged me back to reality. "I'm afraid I don't have time today." I met her gaze. "Do you remember Brent saying anything about Buddy's murder that might help us?"

She swallowed and closed her eyes. When they opened, they were bright with fear. "Brent used to talk about the Amish—make negative comments about our kind. That was one of the reasons I never gave my heart to him." She lowered her voice to a whisper and I bent closer to hear. "He said it was because of the Amish his brother was dead. That's all I remember."

I quickly absorbed the information, but was unable to draw a conclusion that would help the case. Although I had a nagging feeling it was all relevant.

I rose and pulled one of my business cards from my pocket. I handed it to her. "If you remember something else, feel free to call me anytime."

She nodded and stared at the card. Her suddenly gloomy appearance gave me the feeling she wanted to say more. I hesitated on the porch.

"I hope he's all right—Brent I mean." She looked up, frowning. "I didn't mean to hurt him."

"It's not your fault you didn't feel the same way he did. Truth be told, you made a wise choice. Leaving your family

and your culture would have made life very difficult for you."
I shrugged. "Men seem to have a hard time getting over their
first loves."

"Oh, I wasn't his first love." She shook her head and her
mouth thinned.

"Who was then?"

"Samantha Prowes—his brother's wife."

11

Isaiah Coblenz stared at me over the rim of his glasses, the tool he'd been smoothing the leg of the chair with poised in the air. Seth was only a few yards behind him, working on a second, matching one.

"I began two businesses—the building one for my oldest son and the furniture making for myself."

"But you did outbid Brent Prowes several times after he inherited the building business from his brother?" John asked.

Isaiah drew in a sharp breath and set the tool down. He removed his glasses and rubbed his eyes. Wood chips clung to his graying beard.

"At the time, I needed the income for my family. Buddy had monopolized the business in the area. When he was gone, I finally had the opportunity to branch out—which I did." His gaze shifted between John and Toby. "When my son came of age, he took over the business and now it's his. It's not my fault Brent couldn't make a living with what fell into his lap."

His harsh tone made me raise my brows. Most of the Amish I'd met were reserved when speaking to outsiders, hiding their true emotions. But not this guy. The way his lips curled when he mentioned Brent's name made me wonder if he knew the English man had feelings for his daughter. That would make it personal and worth it for the Amish man to destroy the other's livelihood.

Shards of light streamed in through the glass windows, revealing dust particles floating in the air. I sniffed and sneezed. Toby pulled a crumpled, yet clean, tissue from his pocket and handed it to me.

"It sounds like there was some bad blood between you and Brent Prowes." John scratched his chin. "I'm surprised he's still driving for the community."

Isaiah made a rude snorting noise. "Some others don't mind who drives them to town, as long as it's cheaper than the other guy. It's their decision."

John looked at me with wide eyes. He wanted guidance. I cleared my throat, deciding that it was better to be perfectly blunt with this particular Amish man. "Do you have any thoughts about who might have killed Buddy?"

Isaiah pursed his lips and worked his fingers through his beard. When he found a wood chip, he picked it out and chucked it on the floor. "It's not for me to judge, but it's obvious who had the most to gain from his death—Brent Prowes."

I swallowed down the knot in my throat and wrote Brent's name beneath Samantha's. Now we had two Englishers implicated by Amish people in Buddy's death. I glanced at Toby. His eyes were darting from the doorway to Seth and back to

Isaiah. I got the impression he didn't like being shut up in the back room with them any more than I did.

"Did anything happen that you can remember that would make you think it was Brent, besides the fact that he inherited his brother's business?" John pushed.

Isaiah waved for Seth to join us. "You worked on the crew. Tell the marshals what you told me."

Seth moved forward with the slowness of a man who looked like he wanted to hide under the table.

"Buddy looked down on his younger brother. He bossed Brent around the same way he did the rest of us. I saw it in his eyes that it upset him."

"Earlier when we asked you who you thought committed the crime, you didn't mention Brent," John said.

"That's because I don't," Seth replied.

It was difficult to gauge the man. He'd moved here from Blood Rock, so I felt I had a little bit of kinship with him. His accent was different than Isaiah's and the other Lancaster Amish I'd spoken to. He'd grown up with Daniel. And yet, there was something about his manner that made me think he wasn't being entirely honest. My gut clenched.

"Do either of you know anyone by the name of Jerimiah Suggs?" I asked.

"No, I sure don't," Isaiah said quickly. He turned to Seth and a look passed between them that I couldn't read.

"Maybe Joshua Miller could help them out with that one?" Seth's words were slow and cautious.

John and I turned back to Isaiah. I was sure that John was holding his breath the same as I was.

Isaiah shrugged. "Perhaps."

The name tickled my memory until I exclaimed, "Is this the same Joshua Miller who's moving to Blood Rock?"

Seth took a deep breath and spoke freely this time. "One and the same. You might want to ask him about Jerimiah Suggs." He bent over and resumed work on the chair.

My mind swirled with the freaky coincidence that I'd already met Joshua Miller, trying desperately to pull anything from my memories of the man, other than his good looks and confident demeanor.

John cleared his throat, looking away from Seth, who had abruptly stopped talking to us. When he faced Isaiah, the gray bearded man was waiting. "Do you know anyone else from the community who may have worked with Buddy?"

Isaiah's mouth curved downward and his eyes lifted as he thought. "I remember one other young man. He wasn't from around here."

"Do you recall his name?" John asked.

Isaiah swiveled to Seth and clucked his tongue. "Do you recall the fellow I'm talking about? He was tall and dark haired. I thought you and Lester Lapp were friendly with him."

Seth shook his head, remaining silent.

My eyes narrowed on him, catching the twitch at the corner of his mouth.

"Oh, yes!" Isaiah exclaimed. "Danny Bach was his name. He was an outsider, but he seemed to know our customs fairly well—even took to the language quickly."

John scribbled the name down on his pad.

My heart pounded in my chest so loudly I worried the others could hear it. The blood drained from my head, making me see purple dots.

The physical description of the mystery man, and his similar name were too much to be a coincidence.

Danny Bach could be no other than Daniel Bachman, my fiancé.

12

I tapped the eraser end of the pencil on the desk as I stared at Bobby Humphrey, Blood Rock's coroner and my go-to guy on ethical issues. He fumbled through the stack of files on his lap, searching for one in particular. He stopped and looked up.

"What has that pencil done to you—or are you trying to drive me into an early grave with that incessant tapping noise?" he growled.

I chewed on my bottom lip and thudded my head against the back of my chair. Bobby set the files down and softened his tone. "What's wrong, Serenity?"

I'd known Bobby since I was a kid in pigtails. Sometimes it was weird being his boss.

I stood up, crossed the room and peeked into the hallway. The coast was clear. The department was unusually quiet. Normally, I would have been relieved, but today, the lack of anything to do made my mental state even more fragile. I seriously needed a distraction—I even would have welcomed a visit from the former sheriff, Tony Manning.

I closed the door and passed by Bobby and his arched brows. I sat back down, leaned across my desk and rested my chin on my hands. "In all the years you've been in law enforcement—" I sucked in a breath "—have you ever found out something about a person who was close to you, something they had kept secret, something that might implicate them in a serious crime?"

He ran his fingers over his mustache. "Is this hypothetical or have you found yourself deceived by a friend?"

Bobby had the knack of turning questions around. I grunted. "Bobby, this is important. Have you dealt with a situation like that before?"

He scratched his head. "There's been a couple of times in my career when I protected a friend from the law, but their crimes were more of an embarrassment to their families, and they weren't a danger to society." He set his files on my desk and inched his chair closer. "Does this have to do with the marshals and their investigation?"

I nodded in a distracted way, looking out the window. With the sun shining and birds chirping, it would have been a lovely day if my world wasn't crashing down around me.

"John and Toby had a meeting to attend at their regional headquarters. They wanted to have their people analyze some of the evidence from the original investigation and do research on the new information we came up with."

"Do they...have enough to make an arrest?" Bobby asked.

I snorted. "No. They have several suspects." I pointed to my fingers as I spoke. "There's the ex-wife. She's an attorney now and seems like a nice lady, but she's hiding something. I can tell. Then there's the younger brother. The vic treated him badly, didn't appreciate him—the list goes on and on. He had the most motive, as he inherited the family business and had a crush on his former sister-in-law. There's also a quiet Amish man, who doesn't seem capable of hurting a fly, let alone shooting a man, and then bludgeoning him to death. But my gut's telling me *he* has a secret. The Lancaster Amish gave us two more names. One is an Amish guy who's moving to Blood Rock as we speak. There isn't any glaring red flag with him, but he's keeping company with some odd fellows. The final name to pop up was someone who worked with the victim for a short time—another person who kept his relationship with Buddy a secret..." I swallowed. "And took on an alias while he was working in Lancaster." I shuddered and took a deep breath. "My biggest problem is I have no sympathy at all for Buddy Prowes. From all the interviews we've conducted, he was a violent, hateful man. There was probably a line of people who wanted to kill him."

"And your heart isn't in this one, is that right?" Bobby asked.

"It was at first. Solving a cold case intrigues me. But the further I delved into this one, the less enthusiastic I felt. All parties involved have moved on. There's been no further crimes—and no threat to the Strasburg community."

Bobby toyed with his mustache. "If the investigation is pursued, will it affect your friend's life?"

"It might." I straightened in my seat and said firmly, "I'm afraid it will."

He crossed his arms. "If you believed it was right to protect your friend, you never would have mentioned this to me. You would have just done it and not looked back. That's the type of person you are. Following the rules isn't as important to you as justice being served. The fact that you're questioning your-self tells you what you have to do. There's a person out there, living his or her life, while another man's was snuffed out. Whether he deserved it or not might not be the issue at all."

"What is the issue then?"

"A simple shooting would indicate a vendetta killing for one thing or another. Brutalizing the body afterwards points to an extremely sick individual—the type of person who *might* lose it again. And if that were to happen, could you live with yourself?"

My eyes teared up and I wiped the wetness away with the back of my hand. My heart pounded and it was difficult to breathe. *Why is this happening?* I screamed in my head.

"Do I have your confidence with this conversation?"

"Of course. I have faith you'll make the right decision, and whatever that decision is, I'll go along with it." I began to open my mouth and he held up his hands. "Please don't tell me anything that will keep me up tonight. It's easier to plead ig-norance if I really am ignorant."

I nodded. "I get it." My cell phone rang and I glanced at the number—Laura's. "Damn. I forgot all about dinner at my sister's."

I stood up and pushed the files aside. "These will have to wait until tomorrow."

"No worries. They aren't going anywhere." He inclined his head. "Perhaps being with family will help you make your decision."

A rap on the door sounded. It opened just wide enough for Daniel to peek in. "I hope I'm not interrupting an impor-tant powwow—" he glanced at his watch "—we're going to be late for dinner at Laura's."

I smiled and tried to ignore the burning in my chest. "I'll be right out." He got the hint and disappeared, shutting the door.

I looked back at Bobby. "Usually being with family does the trick, but I don't think it's going to work this time."

❧

Taylor snuck up behind me, slipping her arms around my waist. I set down the pot I'd been washing and turned around to return the hug. I wasn't a touchy-feely type of person, but I made an exception for my only niece.

"Let me look at it again, Aunt Rennie," she begged, touching the engagement ring.

I held out my finger and she carefully touched it, peering closer. Laura leaned in to take another look. "It's gorgeous." She smiled broadly. "You're a lucky woman."

I pretended to be happy and smiled back. Laura tilted her head and her eyes slightly narrowed. She sensed something was up.

"Taylor, why don't you take the dog for a walk." Her tone was more an order than a request.

Taylor glanced at Zeus, the elderly black lab lying on his furry dog bed in the corner of the kitchen. She rolled her eyes as she grabbed the leash off the hook on the door. "Oh, all right." She looked back at me. "I know when I'm not wanted." Taylor had a flair for the dramatic. She hung her head and sulked before her frown turned up into a grin. "When I get back, I want you to tell me exactly how he proposed. Did he get down on his knees or—"

"Go on!" Laura shooed her daughter out the back door with Zeus.

The dog moved stiffly and I suddenly realized how really old he was. In days gone by, he'd been a rowdy beast and the life of the family. I used to have to fight him off when I'd walk in the front door. Nowadays, he slept more than anything else and I often forgot he was even in the room.

Daniel was in the adjoining room with my brother-in-law and nephew, their voices carrying through the open doorway. Even though we couldn't be overheard, Laura lowered her voice. "What's going on? You've been weird all evening."

I was expecting Laura to see through my act. She was perceptive, and even more so with me. But up until that moment, I hadn't decided how I'd handle her.

Daniel laughed, and the hearty sound of it pinched my gut. I loved him—had agreed to marry him—and now, I feared I didn't even know him.

I smoothed my hair behind my ears. "Is it that obvious?"

"To me it was. I don't think anyone else noticed. You're pretty good at hiding your emotions, so when I see the telltale signs that you're coming unglued, I know it's serious." She stepped closer and squeezed my hand. "This should be a happy time, why are you freaking out?"

Laura was a little shorter than me and where my eyes were gray, hers were light brown. Otherwise, we could have been twins, except for her being five years my senior. Since our parent's deaths, we'd grown closer. Laura had stepped up, filling the void left by Mom. She'd support me one hundred percent, but that wasn't what worried me. Even though I had no idea what would happen with Daniel, I still didn't want her to think badly of him. I couldn't go there just yet, but I needed to talk to someone. If I didn't, I'd go crazy.

I gripped Laura's hand and tugged her into the corner by the refrigerator. "I think I made a mistake accepting Daniel's proposal. He might not be the person I think he is," I whispered.

Laura frowned and glanced towards the doorway leading into the other room. When she looked back, her eyes were moist. "Why would you say that—you love him, don't you?"

I sagged against the counter. "Very much, but love might not be enough." I snorted. "I found out he hasn't been truthful with me about his past—and there might even be legal ramifications. I don't know how I'm going to handle the situation, either."

Her face hardened and she looked a lot like mom. "I've seen how he dotes on you—puts up with your aloofness and the demands of your job. He adores you, Rennie. Don't throw it all away because of your high ideals." She offered a smile. "No one's perfect. Maybe you can look the other way this time."

My brow furrowed as I stared at my sister. She probably thought if Daniel got away, I'd never find a man who'd put up with me. Although she wasn't as focused on justice being served as I was, she was a morally sound person, and her pleading eyes did affect me.

"I won't make a rash decision. I'll gather some more information and then decide." Laura's mouth tightened and I added, "Don't worry, I won't end it unless there's a very good reason. I think if you knew the entire story, you'd see it my way."

She embraced me and whispered into my ear, "Hang in there, it will all work out the way it's supposed to."

"Aunt Rennie?"

I pulled away from Laura and wiped the corner of my eyes.

"Are you heading out, Will?"

He nodded. "I'm going to meet some friends in town."

Will had filled out since the previous fall when he'd left Blood Rock for Montana. It was the trip of a lifetime, one he'd been planning for a while. He would have taken his beautiful girlfriend with him, an Amish girl escaping her life, but he never got the chance. After she'd been murdered, the trip had become an escape from the horror of losing her.

"How long are staying in Blood Rock?"

"For two weeks." He glanced at his mother and back at me. "It's great to see family and friends, and be in familiar territory again, but I've started a life out there for myself. I'm doing well on the rodeo circuit." He smiled faintly and I raised a brow. "And I have new friends out there."

"As in a new girlfriend," Laura teased. She wanted her son close by, but she was trying to remain upbeat about his decision to stay in Montana for the time being.

He was only twenty years old—way too young for the emotional turmoil he'd been through. He'd loved and lost. The resiliency of a youthful spirit was truly amazing. It was good to see him pushing his messy blond hair off his face and smiling again. But it was bittersweet too. If I lost Daniel, I wasn't sure if I'd ever be able to love someone again.

I reached up and tussled his hair. "I'm happy for you. Follow your dreams and live life to the fullest—without doing anything stupid or illegal."

He laughed. "Are you getting sentimental in your old age?"

"Not me. I'm just as cynical as I always was." I shrugged. "It sounded like something a good aunt would say."

He hugged me tightly, and then his mother before he swept out the door.

Laura wiped a tear away and I gripped her shoulder. "At least he's living in a beautiful place. You'll enjoy vacationing out there."

She chuckled and swatted me with the dishrag. I dodged away right into Daniel. One hand caught me, while his other held the cellphone to his ear. My heart stilled at the tense look on his face.

He slipped the phone into his pocket. "Are you up for a drive out to the Amish community?"

"What's happened?" I reached for my purse.

He shook his head. "It's nothing serious, no one's injured or dead." He rubbed his forehead. "It's more of an intervention of sorts. Mervin and Verna need us."

"Us?"

Thoughts of Daniel's connection to the Lancaster community and Buddy Prowes were pushed to the back of my mind. If those kids needed my help, I'd get my shit together.

13

"I don't see what this has to do with us. They're teen-agers—it happens." I looked out the window at the plowed fields, basked in soft moonlight, trying to avoid meeting Daniel's stubborn glances.

"This *is* a big deal. You're right, it does happen, even among Amish teens. But what Mervin did was brave and idiotic at the same time." The level of his voice intensified. "They're going to be shunned."

"Shunned?" My voice rose. "Are you kidding?"

Daniel exhaled. "It might be for a couple of weeks or the entire summer—it's up to Aaron and the ministers to decide. What I'm worried about is that both these kids have been through so much already. Something like this could push them over the edge."

"Why did the boy say anything at all? Did he want to get into trouble?"

"Not exactly. My people are raised with a heightened awareness of their sins—even as kids. They rebel and mess up like English teens. But instead of it being a game to keep their

sins secret, some of them are overcome with guilt over what
they've done."

"Naomi was running around with Eli and Will—she didn't
seem to have a problem with her conscience, and for that matter, neither did Hannah or Mariah. They understood they
were teens and it was expected for them to act out."

"They're not all like that. Mervin is a good kid. He wants
to be with Verna, start a life with her, but he's only sixteen and
still too young, even by Amish standards. I think this was a
desperate attempt at forcing the community to allow them to
be together sooner."

"Do you think he spilled the beans without Verna's con-
sent?" I asked. When Daniel shrugged, I added, "If that's the
case, she might be angry enough to break up with him." I
threw my hands up in the air. "I mean really, who tells their
parents they had sex with their girlfriend? That conversation
only comes up if she gets pregnant."

His brows lifted. "Is that what you did as a teen? Lie to
your parents about what you were doing with your boyfriends
behind their backs?"

My cheeks burned and I opened my mouth, then snapped
it shut. *This isn't the time to confront him about his own lies—and
much more important lies at that. Focus on the problem at hand,* I
ordered myself.

"When I was a teenager, I only had one boyfriend—and
that was Denton. I waited until I was seventeen to lose my vir-
ginity to him. But I guess it was a little too late. He was already
fucking my best friend. Remember, I told you all about it."

He reached over and cupped my hand. I had the urge to
jerk it away, but didn't.

"I'm sorry. I shouldn't have said that. It wasn't right." He paused. "Can't you see how a boy like Mervin would feel the need to unload his guilty conscience?"

The inside of the Jeep was quiet for several long seconds. "I suppose so," I lied. "I still don't see how we can help. This is out of my realm of experience."

"Having an outsider's perceptive can help. I want Mervin and Verna to know they're not alone—they have sympathetic friends."

I stared out the window and heavy silence filled the cab. A row of peonies lined the side of the driveway we pulled into. Their sharp fragrance spilled in through the crack in the window. The pink flowers were muted in the moon's dull light, but I imagined their brilliance in the sunshine. It would have been a nice evening if a couple of kids weren't going to be humiliated in front of their entire congregation because of raging hormones, and my fiancé wasn't somehow connected to a murder that took place years ago. I dug my fingers into the side of my forehead.

Why couldn't I catch a break?

Daniel parked and shut off the engine. I turned the door handle and his hand shot out, grasping my arm.

My head snapped back at him. "Let's get this over with."

His face softened and a smile tugged at the corner of his mouth. "Thanks for coming."

I nodded stiffly and tried to pull away, but he held firm. He leaned over and the smell of musky cologne and warm flannel teased my nostrils. His lips brushed mine and his prickly stubble scraped against my cheek. It was a feeling I usually relished, but not today. I kept up the act to avoid raising his suspicions and kissed him back. My heart wasn't in it, and he knew it. His tongue stalled and his muscles tensed. When he pulled back, he was frowning.

"Is something wrong?" he asked slowly.

"I'm just tired and distracted. You know how that goes."

His expression was distant, as if he were remembering something. My heart thumped and I stared at him, holding my breath.

He inhaled deeply and I drifted closer. The air in the cab was thick with my need to hear Daniel's secrets. I touched his shoulder and he turned to me. The cloud lifted from his eyes and the moment was gone.

"Isn't it great to be a grownup? We can go home later and have as much sex as we want," he said with exaggerated cheerfulness.

I blew out between my teeth and stepped out of the cab. The grass was covered with dew and a whip-poor-will's repeated call interrupted the quiet countryside. Moses and Anna, Daniel's parents, lived in the small white house close to the road. His sister, Rebecca, and her family had the larger farmhouse on the hill. I swallowed down the bitter taste of betrayal and lifted my chin. As difficult as it would be, I had to treat Daniel as a potential fugitive until I had information to clear or condemn him. The thought that he might run had occurred to me and I held on to the thought, even though my heart screamed, *No, he wouldn't do that.* I'd learned a while ago that anything was possible—especially with the Amish. And at the core, he was still Amish.

Daniel rapped his knuckles on the door while I scratched the dog's head, who had greeted us with a wagging tail. He was fluffy and spotted, with one blue eye and the other brown.

Seth Hershberger's puppies popped into my mind and the memory of puppy breath assailed my nostrils.

Moses opened the door, his white beard was long and scraggly, but his dark eyes were surprisingly alert for having unsolicited visitors this late at night.

He grunted. "Haven't we had enough turmoil in the community already? What ill news do you bring us now?"

I saw Daniel flinch and shift a hard gaze to Moses. He was an honorable man, but a grumpy one. And he hadn't forgiven his son for leaving the Amish. After all these years, I didn't think he ever would.

Daniel cleared his throat, refusing to acknowledge his father's words. "We've come to talk to Verna."

Moses stood up straighter. "The girl doesn't need counsel from the likes of you." He stepped closer, but didn't let go of the door. "You'll poison her mind worse than it already is."

My face flushed and I couldn't remain silent. "Now wait a minute. Mervin asked Daniel to come—you can't isolate the boy and Verna." I wagged my finger. "They're crying out for help, and if you ignore those cries, and something bad happens, it will be on your conscience."

Staring at Moses was like seeing an older, gray-haired version of Daniel. They both had the same stubborn features and strong bodies. And right now, Moses was glaring at me with the same look that I'd received from his son on more than one occasion.

His eyes narrowed and he opened his mouth, but before he could respond, Anna pushed by him.

"Aren't you going to invite them in, Mo?" she asked.

His lips pressed together. "I don't think it's a good idea."

Anna was a petite woman and even now, when it was probably past their usual bedtimes, her hair was still pressed up neatly beneath her cap. A spatter of flour smudged her face and her apron was covered with it. She turned to me. "You'll have to excuse my husband, Sheriff. We've been dealing with an unruly teenager. But you already know that and that's why you're here."

"Something like that," I mumbled, glancing at Daniel. His stony stare at his parents showed no emotion. "Sorry to bother you so late in the evening, but after everything those kids have been through, we thought we should come straight over."

Anna wiped her hands on her apron. "I'm finishing up the bread for this Sunday's service. Rebecca is hosting church and I volunteered to help with the sandwiches." She fell silent and looked at Moses.

He threw up his hands saying, "Oh, all right. I'll send the girl out." His face tightened with hostility. "But you two had better not lead her down the wrong path—just see where it got you."

He disappeared through the door, allowing it to slam shut. Anna and I jumped at the noise, but Daniel only shook his head.

Anna reached out and touched his shoulder in an unusual show of affection toward her son. Her hand dropped away quickly enough, but from the surprise that flashed across his face, the small gesture hadn't escaped Daniel's notice.

"You must forgive your father. Verna's defiant spirit is reminding him of the trials he faced with you." She shook her head slowly and stepped up to the porch railing, clutching it tightly. "It wasn't easy for him to lose one of his sons. Now he fears the community will lose both Mervin and Verna."

"The boy is nothing like me," Daniel said harshly. "He's in love, that's all." His tone dropped. "Besides, if he ends up going English, Father won't be the cause of it. Some of us just don't fit into this lifestyle, Ma."

"I understand. There was even a time when I was a young girl and I wondered if my place was here." Daniel's eyes widened. "Falling in love with your father is what sealed my destiny. I only hope Mervin's love for Verna is enough to keep them with us."

She turned to me and picked up my hand. She stared at the engagement ring and then looked up. "It's very beautiful and one of the few customs of the Englishers I envy." She glanced between Daniel and me. "Congratulations. I hope this will settle your restless spirits. Your father won't ever let you know, but he'll be pleased." Anna was an honest and spiritual woman—and she loved her son. I hated the thought of what it would do to her if my suspicions about Daniel were true. "You inherited your rebellion from me, I'm sorry to say, but in all things there's God's purpose. My prayers have been answered—you've finally found your path. I'll get Verna for you," Anna said and went through the door.

The door had barely closed when it opened again and Verna slipped outside. I leaned against the porch railing. The dog pushed its head up under my hand and I continued to stroke it. Verna walked by Daniel, only giving him a curt nod. The girl was usually quite bubbly. Her stoic demeanor showed just how rattled she was.

She stopped in front of me. "I'm afraid for Mervin. He's not going to be able to handle us being separated for so long."

"Daniel explained the situation to me—and about the punishment. A few weeks or even a month isn't that long. Let's not be too dramatic here," I said.

Verna's mouth dropped open and her light blue eyes flashed. She turned to Daniel and rattled off something in Pennsylvania Dutch.

"Are you sure it's been decided?" he asked and Verna nodded vigorously.

Daniel ran his hand through his hair, shaking his head. "No one mentioned that—" he looked at me "—Verna is being sent back to Ohio. Father contacted Jonas Peachey this afternoon. Jonas insisted his daughter move back to Ohio to live with him and his younger daughter, Esta. He says it's time for her to come home."

My head throbbed with the news and just hearing Jonas Peachey's name sent a shiver up my spine. He was a medicine man—the real deal. I'd watched him heal Mervin's injured leg. Something strange had taken place in the Peachey house that day—something I'd never truly understand and I wasn't sure I even wanted to. What stilled my heart now was knowing his abilities in the healing arts and his knowledge of herbal medicines. He had the capabilities of finding out if Verna was pregnant and worse yet, of ending that pregnancy.

I stared at Daniel. "She can't go to him. He may have been cleared of any crimes in our last investigation—" I thrust my chin at Verna "—but if her condition changes, who knows if she'll be safe there."

Verna touched my arm. "Dat would never hurt me." She dropped her voice. "Don't worry. I'm not pregnant. We were careful."

Even in the moonlight, I could see the girl's cheeks turn a dark shade of pink. She dropped her gaze, staring at her feet. "Under the circumstances, I can see why Jonas would want her to return home. She's too young to get married...and if she stays, what you fear might happen," Daniel said.

He had a point. I studied Verna, who was still avoiding eye contact. She was taller than me and like most of the Amish girls, she had an air of maturity about her that English teens didn't possess. I thought of my own niece, Taylor. She was the same age as Verna and yet she still seemed like a kid in many ways. I'd probably lose it if she had a boyfriend *and* was having sex with him. Luckily, my sister was as old fashioned as I was in that department. Taylor hadn't even been allowed to date until she'd turned sixteen a few months ago. She'd grumbled about it in the past, but now that she had the opportunity, she didn't seem as interested in pursuing the boys. She'd developed an independent spirit that reminded me a lot of myself when I was a teen—until Denton had screwed up my life.

I had to remind myself that the Amish culture was different than mine. Finding a suitable mate at a young age was part of their master plan. Marriage at eighteen and a baby the following year was normal for them. It was no wonder that some kids ended up messing around a little early. If Mervin had only kept his mouth shut, the couple would probably have gotten away with it.

Verna looked up. "Dat wanted me to come back anyway. He's marrying Marissa in the fall and he wants us all to be a family." She shrugged. "I'm happy for them. Aunt Ada's death...and everything else...was hard on him—" she raised pleading eyes "—but I didn't want to leave Mervin. He thought we could convince Moses and the other elders to let us marry if we were…you know…" She trailed off and tugged her black jacket tighter around her. "All we did was make matters worse. Bishop Esch is siding with Dat. There's no way I can stay."

I sighed heavily and rubbed my face. Sometimes things were just plain out of my control and this was one of those times. I wanted to help Verna, but she was only sixteen. I couldn't condone a rushed marriage at that age just so they could be together. Sure, they'd probably get married in a couple of years anyway, but it was still the principle. We're only kids once—and those were precious years—even for the Amish.

Daniel was silent and it didn't seem like he had anything to add to the conversation, so I continued, "Will your father allow you to continue dating Mervin long distance?"

Verna's face brightened a little. "Why yes. Dat always liked Mervin. He's already given his blessing for us to be together. He said he just didn't want it to be this soon. He told me on the phone that he'd consider allowing us to marry at seventeen if I came home willingly." I saw the tightness of conflict pass over the girl's face. She looked between me and Daniel. "Please, won't you talk some sense into Mervin?" She stepped closer. "He wants us to run away and become English—" she shook her head "—I don't want to begin our life together on the run, away from all the people we know and love. It would be a mistake. I know it would."

Smart girl. Gazing at Verna now, I saw a little bit of Ada Mae in her. The high cheekbones and wide-set eyes were family characteristics all the Peacheys possessed, but the quick and calculating mind was something she'd inherited from her aunt. I only hoped the demons that had driven the woman to murder and mayhem weren't passed down the line.

I glanced at Daniel. "You'll talk to Mervin about all this, won't you?"

"Of course, but it will have to wait until tomorrow. It's getting late and I don't want to bother Lester and Esther at this hour."

"You won't have to bother them at all." Verna quickly scanned the porch and even peeked into a darkened window. "He's nearby, waiting for me in the old barn on Burkey Road. That's where we usually meet."

My stomach clenched and I shook my head. *You've got to be kidding me.* That was the same barn where I'd been held hostage at gunpoint by Tony Manning while a group of Amish men had deliberated what to do with me. Bad memories, to say the least.

Daniel met my gaze. He knew exactly what I was thinking and he waited for me to nod my head before he replied to Verna.

"We'll go talk to him. I can't make any promises about the outcome though," he said.

Verna came alive and flung her arms around me. "Thank you so much, Sheriff," she whispered into my ear. "He'll listen to you and Daniel." She stepped away, opened the door and disappeared.

The door thudded shut and another whip-poor-will called. I took the porch steps two at a time on the way down.

"Are you all right with going to that barn?" When I didn't immediately answer, Daniel jogged the few steps and grabbed my arm. "Hey, look, I can talk to Mervin on my own. You don't have to go back in there."

His face was strained with concern, but I ignored the look. "I'm a cop, Daniel. Revisiting unpleasant crime scenes is my job."

"But this one was personal. It must make a difference," he argued.

"It's something I need to do anyway. Besides, you dragged me into this soap opera. I want to see how it ends."

A smile spread on Daniel's lips before he dipped down and kissed me lightly on the mouth. "That's one of the reasons I love you so much. You act all tough, but you're really just a softie," he teased.

"That will be my downfall," I muttered, climbing into the Jeep.

14

Moonlight sliced through the tree branches scraping against the side of the barn. The large, rectangular, wooden structure was even creepier looking than the last time I'd been here. Newer boards were nailed up alongside aged wood to keep the barn solid so prying eyes couldn't easily peek in.

It occurred to me as we walked up the dirt tractor path to the front sliding doors that it was ironic that a location used for the elder's secret meetings was also a make-out destination for teens in the community. I wrinkled my nose, glancing up at the cupolas rising from the roof into the starry sky. It certainly wasn't a place I would have picked for a date.

Daniel held his finger to his mouth. The countryside was eerily quiet except for the chirping crickets. The barn sat well off the road, but it didn't really matter as no vehicles had passed anyway. At this hour, most sensible people were already asleep in bed.

"We don't want to scare him off before he knows it's us," Daniel whispered, carefully pulling on the door handle.

I had to admit, being here with him was a lot better than sneaking around the barn by myself. The breeze picked up just as he pulled the door along the track, bending the trees by the barn and breaking the silence with more scraping sounds. It was perfect cover for us to slip into the dark interior and shut the door behind us.

The scent of stale, dry dirt assaulted my nose. It was a smell I'd never forget and I couldn't stop my heart rate from speeding up. Daniel squeezed my hand and I took a quick breath. *This is completely different than when my life was threatened the previous fall,* I told myself. *I got this.*

I followed Daniel, squinting in the darkness to see a pair of old, rusty tractors that looked like they'd been parked in the barn for decades. We passed by a pile of moldy hay that almost made me sneeze. In a few spots, shards of light cut through barn boards and the dusty air, hitting the ground, but otherwise, I was relying on Daniel's night vision to keep us from bumping into anything.

I caught a glimpse of pitchforks and shovels hanging on the far wall, and I swatted away cobwebs that brushed my face. Daniel stopped when the tiny sound of scratching overhead reached our ears. We both tilted our heads, not breathing.

His face touched the side of mine. "Probably a raccoon," he whispered.

I glanced up, hoping if he was right, the little beast didn't drop on our heads.

We went through a doorway that led into the main portion of the barn. This was the place I remembered—a vast open area with nothing but a dirt floor and wooden walls. With the blowing clouds, moonlight came and went, spattering the ground in places below the cupolas.

Daniel pulled me to a stop again. Without letting go of my hand, he raised it, pointing to the corner of the room. In the shadows, I thought I saw movement.

"Mervin! It's me—and Serenity is here too," Daniel called out.

I held my breath. There was a shuffling sound.

"Where's Verna?" Mervin stepped into the light.

"She's fine. We just left her." Daniel let go of me and walked towards Mervin. "It would have been terrible if she attempted to come here tonight and was caught. My father is no fool. He's expecting her to do something like that."

Mervin slumped. "I know, but I wanted to see her." His voice scaled higher.

"I understand. Verna explained everything to us. Hadn't you thought at all about the possibility of your plan going wrong? Once you told your father about you and Verna, he had to go to Moses and Anna since she's living with them."

Mervin dropped to the dirt floor and sat Indian style, burying his head in his hands. Daniel joined him and I reluctantly sat across from them. My fingers brushed the gun holstered beneath my jacket. Call me paranoid, but there was no way in hell I was letting my guard down in this place.

"I didn't think anyone would call Jonas Peachey. The bishop should have kept it Blood Rock business," Mervin grumbled.

Daniel took a deep breath, meeting my gaze before he turned to Mervin. "You made two mistakes here. One was thinking that crossing the line and breaking the rules was somehow going to get you and Verna married, and the other was trusting the adults." My eyes widened, but Daniel didn't see. I forced my mouth to remain closed and listened intently to him when he added, "But remember, you're almost an adult yourself, so you need to start acting like one." He leaned in. "If you and Verna run off at this point in your lives, you won't be able to support her in the outside world. I left when I was nineteen and it wasn't easy at that age. You need the support of family and so does she. If you play your cards right, you might be married by this time next year and building your own house on a piece of your father's farm. You're his child. He wants to help you—if you just give him a chance."

"But we'll be separated." He rolled his head. "I can't be apart from Verna. She's the only good thing in my life. I'm not strong enough."

"You are strong, Mervin. You stood up to your brother when he shot Naomi because you knew in your heart it was the right thing to do." Daniel grunted. "Granted you've had a rough go of it lately, but there's a bright future ahead for you and Verna. You must do the right thing and let Verna go back to Ohio. You'll be allowed to visit her. Jonas is a man of his word. If he said Verna can marry at seventeen, it's simply a countdown to her birthday."

"It won't be simple," Mervin said in a trembling voice.

"Love never is—" he caught my eye "—but it's well worth it."

Daniel stood up and offered me his hand. I let him pull me up and then he turned to Mervin, slapping him on the back. Daniel winked at me before he began conversing with the Amish boy in Pennsylvania Dutch. I didn't mind. It made sense to make Mervin comfortable and at the same time, remind him of who he really was—an Amish teenager.

I let the guys pull ahead of me and paused in the threshold of the doorway leading into the large, empty room. I looked over my shoulder and imagined the scene that used to give me nightmares. At the time, I really thought I was going to become a murder victim myself. Now I knew the Amish in the community better, but I still didn't completely trust them. One thing I'd learned during my investigations of the Plain people was that just like everyone else, they had dark secrets—even Daniel.

But just a few moments ago, I'd witnessed Daniel being the Daniel I'd grown to love. He was a compassionate man, and he'd proven himself to have a high set of morals. It was difficult to believe that he was involved with Buddy's murder. But he'd lied about knowing the man, and it had all happened just after he'd left the Amish. Who knows what his state of mind was at the time.

I swallowed and closed my eyes, trying to slow my pounding heart.

The hand on my shoulder made me jump.

"What are you doing?" Daniel asked.

"Just remembering," I said.

"Why would you want to relive those kinds of memories?"

"Some things are best never forgotten. It keeps a person from becoming complacent and trusting too much."

Daniel furrowed his brow, but chose not to argue with me about it. "We're going to give Mervin a lift home. Come on."

He held out his hand and I licked my lips and took it. Even though his touch was warm, I shivered.

Soon enough I'd discover the truth about Daniel. I willed myself to be patient and enjoy the ignorance while it lasted.

15

"I'm surprised you aren't following this lead with Daniel's assistance." Todd took his eyes away from the road. It was long enough for me to see his brows rising above his reflective sunglasses.

"He's busy on a job," I lied. "Do you have a problem helping me out on this one?" I snapped.

He snorted. "Of course not. I was just asking." He shook his head. "What put you in such a foul mood?"

I avoided looking at him, instead focusing on the passing farms. It seemed for every sunny day, we had two rainy ones. Today, the sky was overcast and threatening rain.

I'd known Todd since middle school. He was my first deputy and a friend. But I wasn't about to mention what was going on with Daniel. Until I had a break in the case that pointed a finger at my fiancé, I would keep my own secrets.

"These Amish cases are always frustrating. Just when I'm closing in on the bad guy, another suspect pops up and I have to start all over." I glanced at Todd. His hair was freshly buzzed and his face cleanly shaven. He seemed more relaxed than usual and I couldn't help commenting on it. "Isn't Heather's due date next week?"

A smile crept onto his face. "Yeah. Very soon I'm going to be a daddy."

"You seem awfully calm. Are you taking pills or drinking a lot of tea?"

He shook his head roughly. "You're so dammed cynical. How do you live with such a pessimistic outlook on life?"

"It's a valid question. Not so long ago, you were a basket case about the unplanned pregnancy and rushed wedding. What's changed?" I was genuinely fascinated with Todd's transformation in the past few months. He was like a different person. He rarely made rude comments to me and I would classify his overall attitude as subdued.

"Having a child changes a person. It finally sank in that I've begun the second chapter of my life. And you know what? It's even better than the last one."

"Married life does seem to suit you well," I admitted.

He laughed. "Heather and I had lived together for so long, I didn't think it would make a difference if we made it official—but it did. Something changed. She's happier, more easygoing so to speak, and that's affected me. I don't know why I didn't pop the question sooner."

"We all wondered that." I grunted and my eyes flicked to him. "Why is it some men wait until a baby is on the way to make a commitment?"

"Daniel didn't." He smirked, revealing a little of his old self. "Unless there's a bun in the oven I don't know about."

"Hell no!" I exclaimed, and then dropped my voice. "Daniel is a different sort of man, that's for sure. I wish he'd slow down a bit."

"I'll admit, I wasn't sure about him at first." Catching my questioning look, he added, "I mean, he was a nice guy and all, but his past made me wonder if you'd be happy with him in the long run. If you're born Amish, you might physically leave, but it's always in his head—if you know what I mean."

"Yeah, I get it. Daniel has his Amish moments, but that traditional upbringing helped make him into the man he is today. He'd never go back to that way of life." I stared out the window, muttering, "At least I don't think he would."

"You're safe, Serenity. He adores you and he knows you'll never put on one of those frumpy, polyester dresses and cover your hair with a stiff white cap."

"I wear a hat every day on the job—what's the difference?" I raised an eyebrow at him.

Todd was about to respond when his hand went up and he pointed at the road. "I do believe we're heading in the right direction."

I followed his gaze to the line of vehicles in front of us. Two moving trucks led the way, followed by two pickup trucks pulling livestock trailers. The best I could make out as we rounded the curve was the first trailer contained cows and the one directly in front of us held several dark-colored horses. A Pennsylvania license plate was on the trailer in front of us.

I sat back. "Sure enough. We've found our man."

We parked along the driveway and waited. When the last horse was pulled off the trailer, I flung the door open and headed straight for Joshua Miller. A little girl took the lead rope attached to the tall horse from him and led the prancing animal toward the barn. He bent down to a second, even smaller girl and gently shoved her in the direction of the house where a round, gray-haired woman waited. The woman called out in Pennsylvania Dutch, waving her hand at the girl. I thought I heard the name Sylvia, but wouldn't bet any money on it. The child ran across the yard with a brown dog loping beside her.

Joshua was shouting out orders to several men who had gathered around him. A boy was tapping a large pig with a long stick and when the animal turned suddenly, he fell into the mud. Joshua ran over and helped the boy up and thrust his hand out for the kid to chase after the pig. I couldn't understand anything anyone was saying, but I didn't need to. They'd obviously moved the entire farm to Blood Rock.

Todd leaned over. "Maybe this isn't such a good time to bother the man."

My eyes narrowed when Lester and Mervin appeared from the side of the cow trailer. Bishop Esch and Moses were with them, assisting with the corral chute for the cattle to be unloaded. About a half dozen black buggies were parked a little ways up the driveway in front of another barn. I exhaled loudly. Figures. Most of the community had already arrived to welcome the newest member of the church.

Even for all my reservations and worry the night before, Daniel had managed to get me into a romantic mood when we'd finally gotten back home. Even now, I could still feel the touch of his hands on my breasts and the taste of his lips on mine. This investigation couldn't wait. I'd lose my mind if I didn't get some answers soon. To hell with inconveniencing Joshua Miller. I wasn't putting it off until John and Toby got back into town either. I couldn't take the chance that evidence would come to light that would incriminate Daniel before I had the opportunity to speak with him first. Things could spiral out of my hands quickly if I wasn't careful.

"Trust me. This is too important. I have to talk to Mr. Miller today," I said bluntly, not meeting Todd's eyes.

Bishop Esch was the first to spot me. He stared for a moment before walking to Joshua. I saw him point in my direction, say a few words and then go back to helping the others with the cattle.

Joshua strode over, frowning. I straightened under his hard look, adjusting my sunglasses.

"Sheriff Adams—is that correct?" Joshua said before he even reached us.

I nodded, studying the man's tall physique. He stood confidently, reminding me of Daniel or the bishop. His beard and hair were thick and light brown, and his features sharp—almost wolfish.

I drew in a short breath. "Mr. Miller, I'd like to ask you a few questions if you don't mind."

He raised his hands and lifted his chin to the side. "I'm really busy here, Sheriff. Can it wait until another day?"

Most people were a little curious about a visit from the law, unless they had something to hide. I stared at the Amish man, trying to gauge his complete lack of interest in my visit. *Had the bishop already mentioned the Buddy Prowes' case to him or did he have a guilty conscience?*

"No, it can't wait." I motioned towards the cruiser. "It will be quieter in the car."

Joshua smacked his lips and his cheek twitched. He walked past us to the car. Todd lifted his brow high at me and mumbled something unintelligible.

Once we were seated, I turned sideways and looked back at Joshua. His face was rigid, like a sulky goat, reminding me of when I'd questioned Eli Bender in the backseat of a car. I certainly hoped this interview went smoother than that one had. Feeling a sense of urgency for Daniel's sake, I didn't waste time on niceties or psychological manipulation. "Did you know Buddy Prowes?"

A small smile cracked on Joshua's face and then was gone. "I know *of* the man, but not personally."

I took a moment to think about the best way to proceed while giving the Amish man some time to become rattled. I didn't really think this particular guy would slip up. He was way too cool for that. After a mutual stare down, I decided the best way to deal with such an arrogant man was to soften my approach.

I removed my sunglasses and lightened my tone. "I'd really hoped you might be able to help me with the investigation. You live in my backyard now—" I shrugged "—we're almost neighbors."

His narrowed gaze flicked from my hair back to my eyes. If the man played poker, he'd be good at it. I couldn't read him at all through his stoic expression. But when he spoke, I knew I'd played my cards right.

"I don't understand why the sudden interest in the case after so many years." He leaned back and inclined his head. "Everything I've heard, Buddy wasn't a nice man. Why are you his champion?"

The question startled me and I pulled back.

Todd barked out, "A murder was committed. It's our job to find out the truth, even if the victim wasn't likable. Assholes have rights too."

My stomach clenched as I looked at Joshua. His lip curled up to the side. He knew he'd hit a nerve and he was enjoying it. I'd have to tread carefully with him. He wasn't an ordinary Amish man. He was as sure of himself as the bishop was, but without the pious nature. He felt superior to outsiders and he didn't bother to hide his feelings. I had no idea if he had any connection to Buddy's murder, but I was certain the man would stir up trouble in Blood Rock if given the chance.

I ignored Joshua's question all together, not giving him any power in the interview. "One more thing before you go— do you know a Jerimiah Suggs?"

His face didn't change expression and he remained quiet for long enough that tension filled the cab. I caught a glimpse of someone walking by the car and Todd moaned. We exchanged glances and I rolled my eyes. This day had just managed to get worse.

Joshua smiled slightly and I got the feeling he was about to throw me a bone. "I knew a man who used to be called by that name, for a short time."

I raised my brows and leaned over the seat, holding my breath.

"Jerimiah went English for a while. He changed his name back to his birth name went he returned to our people." Joshua looked back at me with a smug little grin.

He'd purposely said *our people* to let me know in clear terms where his allegiance was. He'd just drawn a line in the sand.

"Okay. What's he called now?" I lifted my chin, fighting down the butterflies erupting in my belly.

"Stoltzfus—Jerimiah Stoltzfus. At the time he was an outsider, he purchased a rental building just over the county line into York. It's my recollection some young Amish men stayed there—something of a boarding house you can say."

"Did you live there?" I asked.

He snorted and cleared his throat. "No. Unlike the others, I wasn't a lost soul, searching for freedom from my community."

I quickly digested what he'd said. Now other possibilities were beginning to nudge and prod me. I stopped him when he gripped the door handle.

"You said only one more question." He looked up with a twinkle in his eye that I found unsettling.

"I lied." I pointed out the window. "Why is *he* here?"

I realized I'd given too much of my personal feelings away when Joshua's gaze followed mine and then he looked back. "The lower forty acres of my property, I bought from Tony Manning. He's going to walk the fence line with me and point out a spring that's covered with bushes," he said, his rough, low voice straining to sound sweet.

I nodded and followed him out of the car before Todd could say anything.

"Sheriff." Joshua tipped his straw hat and grinned. "I'm sure we'll be seeing a lot of each other now that we're neighbors and all."

I nodded, but remained tight lipped, watching him walk away and begin shouting orders out to the men waiting beside the trailer.

"He's a prick, isn't he?" Todd sidled up to me.

"Yeah...and unfortunately, a smart one," I muttered.

"Come on. Let's get out of here before there's trouble," Todd said. There was a hint of pleading in his voice as he nudged me.

"Wait for me in the car. I have someone else I need to talk to."

"I was afraid you'd say that." Todd shook his head, but left me.

Tony had already glanced over at me several times, but this time, seeing me standing alone and staring back at him, he made his move.

When he approached, I noticed his blue eyes looked even lighter in the sunshine. He was a big guy and I had to crane my neck to look up at his face. If he lost thirty pounds, he'd be Clint Eastwood's twin. A fact that had helped build up his reputation as a dude not to be messed with in Blood Rock, even before he became sheriff.

He smirked. "It's nice to see you out of that stuffy little office of yours and mingling with the common folk."

I choked down several comebacks. Tony liked to rile me, and I wasn't going to give him the satisfaction of knowing he'd succeeded. Plus, I just didn't have the energy for an argument at the moment, and I was still distracted by the information Joshua Miller had provided me and wondering why he'd been so helpful.

"It's nice that you have remained in contact with the Amish people," I commented, looking past him as the first cows jumped off the trailer and into the chute.

Tony moved to my side, observing the same scene before he glanced down. I caught his gaze.

"They're an interesting people—best neighbors you can have. But I never forget they have their own agenda, *always*." I tilted my head and my heartbeat slowed. Tony didn't bother to lower his voice. Everyone was busy, jogging here and there to unload animals and carry boxes to the house. "They aren't much different from you and me, really. They try to do the right thing, but many of them hold grudges." He smiled as though he knew a secret. "I learned a long time ago how competitive they really are. They know jealousy is a sin, but many of them covet each other's farms, livelihoods, horses and even wives." When he saw my brow lift above my sunglasses, his smiled deepened. It wasn't a friendly gesture, more of a sinister look that sent chills down my spine. "When you're aware of their true natures, and open your eyes wide enough, you'll see who has it in for who. And *that's* the person you want to talk to when you're looking for answers."

I opened my mouth, but Tony turned away and joined the others at the corral.

The gloomy weather matched my mood when I walked to the cruiser and climbed in.

"How did that go?" Todd asked carefully.

"Maybe Tony ate his happy cereal this morning." I glanced over at Todd. "He gave me some advice. And for a change, I think it might actually help."

16

"Do you really have to go back to Pennsylvania today?" Daniel sat on the bed as I threw my clothes into a duffle bag.

The sky outside the window was still hazy dark, but to the east it was brightening. I hated getting up so early, but when I'd received John's text message about meeting in Strasburg that morning, I couldn't say no. I contacted Todd and rearranged my schedule. Now all I had to do was get away without Daniel trying to come along.

"Yeah, it's bad timing, I know. We have one more lead to follow up on."

"Can't the marshals handle it on their own?" His voice rasped.

I paused from stuffing a shirt into the bag. "Sure. But I want to follow through on this one." I saw the hurt on Daniel's face before he looked away. I felt breathless. "So you never spent much time in Lancaster?"

His head snapped up. "Like I said before, I've been there."

His vague answer heated my cheeks and made me queasy. The last thing I wanted to do was lose it and say something that would indicate that I knew he was lying. But I decided to take a chance and trust him a little. After all, we were engaged and other than him lying about knowing Buddy, I didn't have any evidence he had taken part in the crime in any way.

"Joshua Miller is a haughty guy, isn't he?"

"Josh isn't so bad. He's the first one to show up when someone needs help. He just never questioned being Amish. It always made sense to him." Daniel raised a defiant eyebrow. "I always envied his steadfastness."

I stared at him, trying hard to keep my facial expression bland. I'd only mentioned Joshua Miller to him in passing after I'd seen the man talking to Elayne, Moses and Tony at the diner. How could Daniel know so much about an Amish guy from Lancaster if he didn't admit that he had indeed lived there for a while?

I didn't want him to know he'd just messed up, so I quickly continued, "He said that Jerimiah Suggs is actually Jerimiah Stoltzfus. I guess the guy left the Amish for a while and changed his name."

Daniel refused to acknowledge what I'd just said. The quiet in the bedroom was so complete I feared he could hear my heart beating.

I waited, the pain in my gut twisting even more.

When he looked up, his face was scrunched. "I wish you wouldn't go."

Daniel wasn't the type of guy who showed his vulnerability often. The fear lighting his eyes made my heart skip. I wrapped my arms around him and he grasped my hips and pressed his cheek against my breasts.

"I'll be back tomorrow—the next day at the latest. It's not a big deal," I murmured into his hair.

"A lot can change in a couple of days," he said and I froze in his arms. He added, "When your woman is a cop."

His last statement didn't make me breathe any easier. Daniel knew I was close to finding out the truth about Buddy Prowes, and he was afraid.

I glanced up at the rapidly moving clouds. The wind was sharp and the air was charged with energy. The trees framing the front of the two story, rectangular building were bent low, their branches scraping the siding. The metal sign at the curb, STOLTZFUS BED AND BREAKFAST, snapped back and forth with *clinking* noises.

"So now it's a tourist attraction," I mumbled, glancing at Toby.

He lifted a brow. "Can't blame them. On a full night, this place probably brings in a fortune."

John spread his arm wide, directing me up the porch steps first. I didn't waste any time going through the door.

The walls and floor of the room were lightly stained wooden boards. A countryside painting with a horse, buggy and a farmhouse was displayed on one wall and a colorful woven rug took up much of the floor space. An Amish girl sat behind the desk in the corner. She looked up, smiled brightly and then called out in her language. The woman who bustled through the arched doorway wore a pretty blue dress, but her apron was stained and her face was smudged with flour. She held out a tray of pastries to us and said, "Good afternoon. Looks like you made it before the stormy weather arrives."

John glanced at me with a confused look, but I immediately understood what was going on.

"You mistake us for your guests. We're actually here to talk to Jerimiah Stoltzfus. Is he around?" I asked.

The woman's face grew wide. "Oh, so sorry. I have six rooms booked for tonight for the wedding tomorrow. I just assumed you were here to stay the night with us." She extended the tray out further. "Take a desert anyway. Jerimiah is out back. He's trying to fix the lawn mower—and I do mean *trying.* That machine has given us fits for years. I think it's high time to buy a new one, but oh no, Jerimiah likes to tinker with the contraption." She leaned in and covered one side of her mouth. "This time I think the mower has got the best of him. I already called the shop and told them to be expecting us in a day or two."

I returned her smile and plucked a turnover from the tray. Toby followed suit and so did John, only a little more reluctantly.

"Thank you. They smell delicious," I gushed.

"You got an apple one." She turned to Toby and John. "Yours are raspberry."

"Are you talking about Miriam Coblenz's wedding?" I asked, biting into the warm pastry.

"Why yes—are you friends?" The woman's eyes were sharper now as she inclined her head.

"We met last week." I lifted my shoulders. "She mentioned she was getting married."

The woman shook her head. "It's about time if you ask me." Again she leaned over and lowered her voice, even though the only other people in the room were the marshals and the girl. "For such an attractive woman to be a spinster until the age of thirty-four is unheard of around here."

I didn't say anything. I was thirty-four—and I'd just become engaged. The apple and sugar melting in my mouth didn't erase the sour taste her words had made.

Toby interrupted, probably fearing I was about to make a cutting remark. "This is the most delicious thing I've ever eaten."

The woman smiled deeply at him, her cheeks flushing. Over her shoulder she said, "Leanne, take these lovely people out to your father." She turned back to us. "You better hurry, rain's coming."

With a swish of her lavender dress, the girl rounded the corner and we had to stretch our legs to catch up with her. We followed her down a long, narrow hallway and through a screen door that she flung open.

Without a word, she pointed toward a shed and then ran past us back into the house.

"Friendly child," John commented.

"The girls are usually shy. Don't take it personally," I said.

"The mother certainly wasn't a shrinking violet." Toby snickered.

I agreed with him, but didn't bother to respond. John was already shaking hands with Jerimiah.

"This is Serenity Adams and Marshal Bryant. Do you have a minute?"

The man straightened up from the mower and wiped his oily hands on his pants. He was short, overweight and sweating profusely. But the smile on his round face was genuine.

"Of course." He nodded at the mower. "In a way, you're rescuing me."

Toby removed his hat and scratched his head. "I didn't think your people used lawn mowers."

Jerimiah's brow furrowed and then he laughed. "Did you think we cut it by hand?"

Toby shrugged and glanced at me and John. I smiled behind my hand.

The Amish man reached over and slapped Toby's back. "No worries. Our ways are often misunderstood. In our community, push mowers are allowed, but no riding ones."

"What's the difference between the two?" Toby couldn't let it go and I shot him a murderous look.

Jerimiah twisted the end of his black beard between his fingertips. "It's been a part of our Ordnung for as long as I remember." He pursed his lips. "Riding mowers are like cars. We'd get into all kinds of mischief if we had access to those."

We stared back at Jerimiah and briefly, he managed a still face. Then his lips twitched and he barked out a loud laugh and doubled over.

I raised my brows at John, who merely shrugged. He shot Toby a warning look when Jerimiah finally faced us again.

The wind gusted and I zipped up my jacket, glancing at the darkening sky.

John must have noticed the changing weather too. "Did you know Buddy Prowes?" he rushed out.

The abrupt question made the smile disappear from Jerimiah's face.

"Yes, I recall the man. He died a long time ago," he said quietly.

"We've reopened the case. The crime was exceptionally brutal. Were you at all afraid of a murderer on the loose in the area?" John asked.

Jerimiah's brown eyes glanced upwards, indicating that he was trying to remember. If they'd gone down, I would have thought he was fabricating a lie.

"No, no. I don't remember anyone being fearful for their lives." He looked away and then back again. "Buddy was the type of person who we all thought would come to a violent end."

His blasé attitude bothered me. "Kind of like, he lived by the sword, and therefore he was going to die by one. Is that what you mean?"

Jerimiah nodded unabashedly. "That's right. It wasn't a surprise."

"Did you work for Buddy?" John asked.

"Oh no—I'm not a builder." He swept his arms wide. "I bought this place when I was quite young. It was before I married, so I rented the rooms to other young men like me."

"At the time, you weren't Amish, is that correct?" I crossed my arms.

Jerimiah's eyes widened and his mouth dropped open, but he recovered quickly. "It's no secret. I left for a while and then came back. Some of us do that."

I caught John's encouraging glance and continued the questioning. "Did anyone on Buddy's work crew rent here?"

"Several did. Let's see, there was Lester and Seth, but neither one of them stayed long." John had his notebook out and was writing, so I didn't have to. "And Danny Bach."

"There's that name again," John said, scribbling it down. "Something about it strikes me as familiar."

I found it difficult to breathe, but I forced the air out. Lightning zigzagged across the sky and raindrops began to fall.

"Oh, and then there was Brent Prowes."

My head snapped up. "Brent lived *here?*"

Jerimiah nodded, holding his hat firmly to his head as another gust of wind pummeled us. He began inching towards the backdoor and I stopped him.

"For how long?"

"Only a few months. I kicked him out."

"Why?" John had found his voice.

"Because he killed my dog."

The rain came down harder and Jerimiah hurried up the back steps. I glanced between John and Toby, and their expressions revealed they felt the same way I did.

"Hey, do you have any rooms available for tonight?" John said as we followed Jerimiah through the doorway to escape the pouring rain.

Jerimiah took his hand off and waved it in the air to dry it. "Martha, how many rooms are vacant?" he called out.

Martha answered from the other room. "Two!"

"Perfect." John pulled out his wallet. "I'm booking them for the rest of the week."

I looked out through the streaked window at the watery, green world, feeling confusion, hopelessness and betrayal.

If Daniel was completely innocent, why would he keep this part of his life secret from me?

17

"I don't like it." John frowned.

"It's a good plan. Serenity can handle herself," Toby argued. "Besides, I'll be in there with her. I won't let her out of my sight."

John's eyes drifted to the tight, cleavage revealing shirt I'd bought at the Fashion Barn a couple of hours earlier. I tugged it up and glared back at him. "This is the only way Brent might open up. If he even gets a whiff of the law, he'll never say a word. I've worked cases with guys like him. He won't talk to us if we approach him directly."

"That might be true, but we can't control the variables inside a bar. Anything can happen." John continued to frown.

"Sure we can." Toby leaned in between me and John from the back seat and thrust the notepad at John. He pointed to the drawing of the interior of the building. "I already cased the joint. There's only one main entrance—and that's the front door. You can stay parked here and monitor anyone who goes in or out. The back door is in a room behind the counter, and it's locked. I'll be in there with her. She'll be fine."

"But she's not a marshal," John reminded us.

"No, but she isn't doing anything to entrap him." He winked at me. "And if things go south, I'm sure she can handle herself. She is a sheriff after all."

John exhaled, running his hand through his hair. "I don't doubt you're perfectly capable of taking care of yourself and anyone else in there—" he met my gaze "—I just don't want any mistakes that might risk us getting a conviction on this guy if he is our perp. Do you both understand that?"

I nodded. "I'm just going to have a casual conversation with him. He won't suspect a thing."

"I hope you're right. If anything goes wrong in there, it'll jeopardize our jobs."

I looked back out the window. The rain had slowed to a drizzle, but the parking lot was still full of puddles. The Backstreet Bar wasn't much different from Charlie's Pub in Blood Rock, except that Charlie's had a quaint, small town ambiance that made it seem less seedy. This place was a mixture of a biker bar, truck stop sort of establishment that gave me the impression that a lot of its patrons were transients. The two small windows out front were shuttered up and the only lights shining were from the Budweiser and Coors Light signs. My eyes settled on the dented, gray pickup truck across the lot.

I'd had Todd track down Brent's house and when we arrived there, I called him back to run the license plates of the truck parked out front. We followed him to the bar and then drove across town to Yoder's Smorgasbord Restaurant. Lucky for us, Tonya had been working and she'd told me that Brent would probably spend the entire evening at the bar. It was over a quick dinner that Toby and I had come up with the plan for me to go undercover to talk to Brent.

Jerimiah had told us the story of how Brent had become angry with his golden retriever for not coming to him when he called him one day. An hour later, Brent went outside and Jerimiah caught him beating the dog with a piece of lumber off the work truck. The dog died in Jerimiah's arms and he'd ordered Brent off the property for good. I'd asked him why he hadn't called the police and pressed charges, and he'd only stared at me dull-eyed, saying Brent had been drinking all day and had been depressed about girl troubles. The Amish man didn't have the heart to have Brent arrested.

I pressed my lips together tightly. It would be difficult to play the part of a friendly woman looking for a good time with a man who would kill a dog in cold blood. Unlike Jerimiah, I didn't believe there was any excuse to do such a thing. I'd had to shoot an attack dog once that was turned loose on me and Daniel, and even though I had no choice, I still hated doing it—and I hated its owner, Asher Schwartz, for putting me into the position even more.

But the fact that this guy had it in him to do such a thing made it feasible that he could have also killed his brother in a fit of rage. Jim Allen had written Jerimiah's name down in the file for some reason—maybe he was following the same leads we were.

"You have to be delicate with this guy. If he did murder his brother, he must have been fairly stealthy to get away with it all these years." John looked at me harder. "He's dangerous, Serenity. Don't take any chances with him. See what you can find out and bring the information back to me. That's it. Oh, and you had better remove your engagement ring."

I nodded, quickly glancing away. What John didn't understand was that I had entirely selfish reasons for being so invested in the case. Daniel had something to do with it and until I figured out exactly what his involvement was, I was going to try to protect him.

♫

"I'll have a Long Island Iced Tea," I told the bartender.

A ZZ Top song was playing on the jukebox and cloud of cigarette smoke stung my eyes. About a dozen large, tattooed men were at the pool tables. Some were leaning against the dark wooden walls and others gripped billiard cues in their hands. Several women mingled with them. They held mixed drinks, wearing a variety of sleazy, tight clothes. I couldn't help wrinkling my nose at the cheap perfume permeating the air.

I sipped my drink and swallowed, glancing down the bar. Two men were already engaged in conversation with a pair of young women who looked barely old enough to be in any bar, let alone a shady joint like this one, and another, gray-bearded man stared at the bottle of beer in front of him, too drunk to even talk. But the guy at the end of the bar, sitting kitty corner to me, caught my eye. I'd studied enough pictures of Buddy Prowes to see the family resemblance and was betting he was my guy.

The man was tall, wiry and dark haired. He sported a short-cropped black beard and a deep frown on his face. I stared at him for a moment, but he didn't return my look, so I shifted my gaze back to Toby, who sat in the corner of the bar. He lifted his chin towards Brent and nodded his head.

My heart began to drum harder and I grunted softly. Early on in my law enforcement career, I'd been called on a few times in investigations to do exactly what I was doing now—look sexy and get a guy to open up about a crime. I never liked doing it. Hell, I didn't enjoy talking to strangers in general, let alone creepy guys who in most cases, I already knew were rapists. Brent didn't fit into that category, but he was now a suspect in his brother's brutal murder—and he'd killed a dog. My stomach clenched as a picture popped into my mind of Brent doing it. It would take all my acting skills to pull this one off. Thank God I'd taken drama class for a couple of years in high school. Mrs. Shumaker had taught me the art of pretending to be someone else. I took another sip of my drink and a deep breath. I was about to become a tipsy, flirty woman.

Picking up my drink, I pushed off the stool and walked around the bar. One of the other men at the bar eyed me up and down, but I ignored him. When I reached the vacant stool beside Brent, I plopped down on it, sitting close beside him.

He finally noticed me. His brown eyes widened and a small smile cracked his lips.

I wasn't proud to admit I could hold my liquor pretty well and the only chance of this fiasco actually working was if I was believable. I swallowed a gulp and set the glass down. It was now only half full, just the way I wanted. A cold chill passed over me when I thought of Daniel and what he'd think of me going undercover this way for the case, but then I dismissed him. It was *because* of him I was in this position in the first place. If I played my cards right, he'd never even know anyway.

"Are you ready for another drink?" Brent asked. His slight smile lingered.

"Yes, sir, I am," I drawled. "I've had a bad day—a really bad day. I plan on having several more." I slumped a little, covered a pretend burp with my hand and fluttered my eyelashes.

Brent flicked his finger at the bartender and a moment later, another Long Island Iced Tea was placed in front of me. "Thanks. That's nice of you." I offered my hand and he shook it. "I'm Serenity."

"Brent." He leaned in. "I haven't seen you in here before."

"It's my first time." I took another sip, this time smaller, and rolled my head. "Actually, it's my first trip to Pennsylvania." I smiled weakly, meeting his gaze. "I can't say it's been much fun."

His brows lifted. "Does it involve a guy?"

I widened my eyes, feigning surprise. "Yeah, sure thing. How'd you guess that?"

He shrugged. "I can't imagine a pretty woman like yourself being so down in the dumps for any other reason." He gulped the contents of his shot glass. "I'm a good listener."

I considered Brent's soft spoken voice and friendly manner and shivered. I hoped he didn't notice and looked away only long enough to spot Toby across the bar. He'd moved, taking the stool I'd vacated.

Brent didn't fool me. I'd been around a lot of guys like him before. They were smooth on the outside, but inside, they were psychotic. The occasional twitch of his lips and his shifting eyes told me that even though he was engaging with me, he was still preoccupied with something else. His posture, leaning over and crowding me, showed he was confident and was used to subtly intimidating people. He probably wasn't that much different from his older brother, Buddy, except that he was able to control his temper better. Miriam was right to stay away from this guy.

I made an exaggerated sigh and turned to Brent. "A couple of months ago, out of the blue, an old boyfriend of mine started calling me. We'd had a rough breakup, so it really surprised me that he'd reached out. I didn't trust him at first, but after a few calls, I loosened up." I licked my lips. "He told me he was living here, so I decided to visit in person." I paused for effect. "I soon discovered he had a live-in girlfriend. What a fool I was." I glanced at Brent. "Why would he be so nice to me when there was no chance at us being together?"

Brent shook his head and then stared at bottles on the shelf behind the bar. I held my breath, waiting to see if my story struck a nerve with him. Were thoughts of Miriam Coblenz, the Amish woman he'd pined for all these years going through his mind? Or was he possibly thinking about his former sister-in-law, Samantha?

He was listening, but his expression betrayed no opinion. "People can be cruel. In my life, it's been the women—the pretty, sweet and meek women—who were the sick ones." His lips pressed together. "A girl did me that way—led me on and then threw me away like I was yesterday's trash."

He took a gulp from his bottle of beer and the vein at the side of his temple protruded. My story *had* gotten to him and now his own angst was fueling the fire.

The muffled sound of an argument at the pool tables reached my ears and I fought the desire to look over and see what was going on.

Brent placed his hand over mine and I froze. It took everything I had not to slam his face onto the counter.

He put his hand on my shoulder and the smell of alcohol wafted from his breath. I tilted my head.

"I have one word that will make you feel better. *Revenge*," he whispered.

My heart pounded in my chest as he started to say more. But the tap on my other shoulder turned me around.

The guy who had ogled me earlier hung over me. His eyes were bloodshot and some foam of his last sip of beer was bubbling on his mustache.

"You've been monopolizing this...pretty lady for way too long. Why don't you give...someone else a go?" The man's words were slurred and my gaze narrowed on him.

Brent leaned back and chuckled. "It's up to the woman to decide who she wants to talk to with. You're too drunk to have any manners."

I stared challengingly at the man who'd interrupted my suspect at the moment he seemed to be about to say something useful. I said with a low, threatening voice, "I'm not interested." I jerked my gaze away and faced Brent.

"Hey, girlie, there's no reason to be a bitch," the man growled into my ear.

I would've been fine if he hadn't placed his hand on my thigh when he'd leaned in. Instincts took over. I swiveled and slid off the stool and brought my knee up into the man's groin. He gasped and bent over, clutching his balls.

A crash sounded behind me and I looked over my shoulder. I ducked in time to avoid the splinter of a chair streaking just a few inches over my head. A redheaded woman screamed, drawing my eye in her direction. A burly man, bare chested beneath a black leather vest, had pulled the young woman into a chokehold. Her makeup was smeared from tears as she tried to punch her captor. Another man of equal statue, with a long, gaunt face, had a handgun pointed at the struggling pair.

The words *What the hell?* flashed through my mind as I bent down to free my own 9 MM from its calf holster beneath my jeans. The game plan had changed. A woman's life and everyone else's in the bar, were in jeopardy. I had no choice but to reveal myself.

But before I pulled my pant leg up, I heard someone shout out, "Freeze, U.S. Marshal!"

Without me even noticing, Toby had left his stool and was only five or so yards from the commotion. His Glock was steady in his hands and aimed at the man holding the gun.

"Drop your weapon!" Toby called out, stepping closer.

People closest to the door ran for it and several others dropped beneath their tables. The bartender was nowhere to be seen and I imagined he was hiding behind the counter.

Two men stood to either side of the gunman and my eyes flicked between them. They each had a hand inside their jacket and I said a silent, *Oh, shit, this isn't good.*

"No one invited a lawman in here—you're out of your jurisdiction, cowboy," the gunman said in a surprisingly level tone for the situation.

"Drop the gun and no one gets hurt. We can talk all about whatever problem you're having when you lower your weapon," Toby said in an equally calm voice. With his cowboy hat and his firearm held out in front of him, he looked like a character from an old western movie.

The gunman laughed and I saw the look pass between him and the man to his left. "I don't think so," he said.

The other man brought his hand out of his jacket and I saw the flash of steel. He lifted his arm, aiming at Toby, but didn't get a shot off. Toby's bullet hit him in the head an instant before the man gripping the woman shoved her aside and pulled his out own pistol. Several shots exploded, *pop pop pop pop.* The men crumpled to the floor. Toby was still standing.

My own Glock was in my hand, but I didn't remember drawing it. The freed woman scurried across the floor to the side of the man Toby had shot. She held his bloody head in her hands. With his gun still out, Toby stepped lightly until he reached the men who'd shot each other. His gun was trained on the only man not shot in the group who stood to the side with his hands up. Toby's eyes flicked between the men and he didn't see the redhead grab up the pistol off the floor.

"You done killed him!" she screamed.

Toby didn't have enough time to reposition to make the shot.

But I did. My vision tunneled on the woman and the familiar black void formed, leading straight into her chest. I fired and the woman fell over on top of the man she had just been holding.

Blood spread out beneath the bodies on the floor.

"What the hell is going on in here?" John shouted from the doorway. His firearm was drawn and his eyes darted around the room.

A woman was crying and a man cursed. Patrons began standing and inching away from the bodies. Sirens wailed outside the bar.

"Everyone, hands up, over to the wall," Toby shouted.

I didn't lower my gun until the police arrived, and then I finally turned back around. Brent was gone.

Toby moved to my side. "Where's Brent Prowes?"

I rubbed my temple, and then pointed at the door behind the bar that was flung open.

"Dammit," Toby muttered.

"So much for being discreet." John frowned at the bodies on the floor.

When the Lancaster sheriff approached us, we flashed our badges. "You three have a lot of explaining to do," he said.

Toby rolled his eyes my way. "It's going to be a long night."

When I glanced back at the empty stool where Brent had sat, goosebumps rose along my arms. I had the sinking feeling in my gut that the worst part about the night was that he'd slipped away into the night.

18

Sunlight streamed in the window, warming the side of my face. Murmurs of quiet conversation and the clinking of silverware on ceramic filled the dining room. I glanced around at the other guests, an English couple and two Amish families, envious of their carefree morning.

John stirred his cup of coffee and looked up. "We caught a lucky break last night."

I brought my cup to my mouth, savoring the warm coffee aroma before I took a sip. I raised a brow and peered over the cup at the marshal. "How so?"

"You two stumbled into a drug turf war. Early this morning the feds called me about the deceased." He nodded his head at Toby, who was paying more attention to his scrambled eggs and pancakes than listening to his partner. "We found out from his fingerprints that the man Toby shot was a fugitive our Los Angeles office has been hunting since 2012. He was involved in another drug deal out west that left three people dead. One of them was an undercover cop." He poured more cream into his cup and stirred. "So you can only imagine how ecstatic law officers from several agencies are that we finally got our man."

I glanced back out the window. A line of colorful Amish dresses hung on the clothes line and flapped gently in the breeze. There had been a steady sound of clip clopping hooves on pavement outside. It was a busy morning in the Amish town.

I set my cup down. "What are the chances that a random, last minute idea to go undercover to talk to Brent Prowes would turn into a shootout where one of America's most wanted was shot dead?"

"Not very." Toby finally joined the conversation. "Maybe we should buy a lottery ticket today."

I ignored his comment and turned to John. "Did you have any problems explaining my involvement in the case?"

Toby's fork paused in front of his face as he looked at his partner.

John blinked and sipped from his cup. "I didn't tell them everything—yet. We have an interview with the feds this morning and another one with the locals this afternoon. It won't be a problem. No one was too concerned with the reason you were in there—they were too busy reveling in the outcome."

"What about the woman I shot? Any news about her?" I asked.

"She had a rap sheet a mile long. Drug charges involving a meth lab in her kitchen and resisting arrest to name a couple. Her kids were taken away from her a year ago when social workers intervened." He offered a small, encouraging smile. "She wasn't a nice lady. The world won't miss her."

"You'd think that would make me feel better." I toyed with the eggs on my plate. "It doesn't."

"You had no choice. She would've shot me dead," Toby spoke up.

I waved my fork in the air. "I have no remorse for killing the woman. She brought it on herself." I shook my head. "It feels like I'm a crime magnet or something. I can't even go into a bar on what should have been a little easy undercover work without having to shoot someone." I pushed my plate away and exhaled. "And Brent Prowes got away."

John crossed his arms over the burgundy table cloth. "With all the hoopla, I never got a chance to ask you if you got any information out of him before all hell broke loose."

I glanced at Toby, who had finally finished eating and put his fork down, his fingers laced in front of him. His eyes darted around the room before they settled on me again.

"I managed to hit a nerve with my made up story. He related with it and even gave me some advice."

"What advice?" John asked.

I flipped my hair back. "Basically that revenge would make me feel better."

"Are you serious?" Toby scooted his chair closer and dropped his voice. "That kind of attitude clearly shows the guy's penchant for violent behavior."

"And that he's not the forgiving type," John added.

I kneaded the back of my neck and frowned. A pair of Amish teens in matching light blue dresses walked by and I paused until they were out of earshot. "Knowing the guy holds a grudge doesn't incriminate him in Buddy's murder. He was about to say more, but didn't get the chance."

"We also have to see what we can find out about Danny Bach. His name has come up twice now and we still don't know a thing about him," Toby said, not realizing his words had made my heart skip a beat.

"That will have to wait." John drank the rest of the contents of his cup and set it down. "I think we should focus on Brent Prowes for the time being." He stared at me. "Toby and I will question him later. It's not safe for you if he finds out you're a sheriff who was playing him. We'll take it over from here."

Daniel's face sprang to life in my mind and I glared at John. "I'm too invested in this case to walk away now. I think we're close to a breakthrough."

"It's going to have to wait until all the i's are dotted and t's are crossed regarding the bar shooting. It'll be a few days before we get all the paperwork done," John said.

"I see how it is. You guys got another fugitive and now you're satisfied." I snorted.

Toby's eyes widened as he shot a hard look at John.

"Stand down, Sheriff. I never said I'm done with Buddy's case, just that it's temporarily on hold," John said stiffly.

"While you're taking care of federal business, I can continue the Buddy Prowes investigation on my own," I suggested.

John shook his head and his mouth thinned into a tight line. "Absolutely not. If the perps last night were only two-bit criminals, we would have all been in serious trouble. It's a warning to step back and take deep breath before we proceed. It's a cold case after all. I only took it up because it was important to Jim, and we had some time on our hands."

My stomach churned and I eyed Toby. His face was frozen in a grim line and I knew I wouldn't get any support from him.

"You're making a mistake. If Brent really did kill his own brother, there's a fair chance he'll snap again. Are you comfortable taking that chance?"

"He hasn't done anything in over fifteen years. I don't think a few days are going to make a difference." He stood up. "You already made your statement to the local authorities. Why don't you go home—we'll call you when we get everything tied up with the bar incident."

I stared up at John. *Was he really dismissing me like I was a child?* My face burned, but I held my tongue.

"Good. I'll see Jerimiah about paying for meals and the accommodations." He turned to Toby. "Why don't you get the files together and meet me in the car?"

"Sure thing, boss." Toby dipped his hat.

John looked back at me. "I'm sorry it went down this way. You helped us out a great deal and I appreciate you investing so much time in our case. Have a safe trip home."

When John rounded the corner, I grabbed my purse and began to rise, but Toby's hand on my arm stopped me. "Hold on a minute." He reached across the table and picked up John's satchel and the file folders strewn out around it. He dropped the files into the leather case and stood up.

"You forgot one," I said, staring at the lone file still on the table.

Toby held up a finger to his mouth, and with his free hand, he flicked the file, pushing it off the table. It landed on the vacant chair. A few papers stuck out.

"Oops, I must have dropped one of the files in my hurry to get back to the sheriff's office and all the exciting paperwork awaiting me there." His fake smile broadened. "I learned a long time ago to always follow through on my instincts. Worst thing that ever came of it was my pride being hurt. Best thing was that I saved a life or two." He dipped his hat. "Until next time."

My heart pounded as Toby disappeared through the door. I looked around to make sure no one was paying attention to me. A small Amish girl about three years old at the nearest table caught my eye. She stopped chewing her food and waved at me with a little hand.

I returned the wave and then she giggled and went back to eating. When no one else was paying any attention, I bent over and snatched the file off the chair. I flipped through it quickly, stopping on the page with Brent's name on it. All his information was there, including his home address. I could have had Todd dig up what I needed to continue the case, but it might have compromised my standing with John if he found out. Toby had given me what I needed to move forward, and in a subtle way, his blessing to do so.

I tucked the folder into my bag and startled when I looked up to see Martha standing there.

"Did you enjoy your breakfast?" She picked up the dirty dishes off our table, balancing them in her outstretched arm.

"Very much. You're a great cook, but then every Amish woman I've met has been," I told her. The two Amish families rose from their chairs and began filing out of the room, chatting on the way out.

"Are you here for the wedding?" I met Martha's gaze and my face must have shown confusion because she went on, "I mean, originally I thought you and the two men were business guests, but when you just mentioned that you're familiar with our cooking, I thought you might be here for the wedding." When I didn't say anything and continued to stare at her, my mind jumping with thoughts, she added, "I'm sorry to pry. It's none of my business."

"The wedding's today?" I mumbled.

"Yes, it is." She glanced at the wall clock. "It begins in about an hour." She thrust her chin at the doorway. "The Schrocks and the Masts are heading over there now. They have a driver with a van and they said I could ride along with them, since Jerimiah has to finish up a few things here and will more than likely be late arriving."

I rubbed my forehead and swallowed, trying to calm my pounding heart. "You're right on both accounts. I came here with my partners for business, but I'm also a friend of Miriam's. I've been so busy I forgot all about the wedding."

Martha lowered her voice and puckered her lips. "Jerimiah said the two you're with are lawmen. Did you hear about the shooting across town last night?"

I furrowed my brow. "For not having television or radio, I'm surprised you know anything about it."

"Seth Hershberger stopped by early this morning with the news. He was on his way to deliver a couple of pups to a neighbor." She blushed, looking embarrassed. "You'd be surprised. News travels quickly around here." She shook her head. "Such a tragedy. The woman's name was Daisy. She used to drive the Amish into town occasionally. But then she got into some mischief and wasn't as dependable, so we stopped calling her. I pity her children." She shook her head. "Some people are self-destructive—they can't seem to help themselves. At least no innocents were hurt this time."

She glanced at the clock again. "Do you mind letting yourself out? I don't want to miss that ride. One of the fellows you were with paid for your room along with his. You can leave the key on the desk—" she tilted her head "—unless you're staying another night?"

Martha's face blurred as her words played over in my mind. *Some people are self-destructive—they can't seem to help themselves.*

I blinked. "I'm not sure about another night."

"The room isn't booked, so if you need it, it'll be available." She tucked a few loose hairs up under her cap as she backed away. "You'll want to arrive at eleven-thirty to catch the end of the service. Dinner is served just after noon."

"I misplaced the invitation—where is the ceremony being held?" I lurched out of the chair.

"It's at the Coblenz's farm. Traditionally, our wedding ceremonies are held at the bride's home. See you there." She smiled and hurried from the room.

I took a deep breath to steady myself. *My imagination was probably just running away from me,* I tried to convince myself. But then I remembered what Toby had said about trusting my instincts and my gut twisted.

I *really* hoped I was wrong this time.

19

I rapped harder on the door. The curtains were drawn up tight and I couldn't see into the house. When no one answered, I jogged down the steps and around the side of the small brick house. I stumbled over a soccer ball in the yard, but caught myself before I fell completely. Tonya had told us she'd taken the kids and moved out. She was living in the next county over with her mother, but it was apparent she hadn't had the time to move all of her things from the modest suburban home she'd shared with Brent before she'd left. Boxes were stacked high in the carport beside several children's bikes.

Having his family move out, combined with Miriam's wedding could be just the thing to set off a man with suppressed violent tendencies. I picked up my pace until I reached the side door. I pounded on it for a moment.

"Dammit," I muttered as I ran back to my car.

When I backed out of the driveway, I deliberated where I should go first, holding my cell phone in my hand. Should I call John and Toby and tell them my fears? I groaned and tossed the phone down on the passenger seat. I needed some kind of proof before I called them in, and that's what decided it for me.

A few minutes later, I pulled into Samantha Prowes' driveway. The sun was high in the sky and I was already beginning to sweat when I stepped out of the car. The grass was thick and green, birds chirped and the pink petunias in the hanging baskets swayed in the breeze. Other than the heat, it was the perfect day for a wedding.

Before I reached the house, Samantha's son came out of the garage. An elderly woman walked with him in direction of a blue four-door sedan parked in the driveway.

"Excuse me," I called out. "Is Samantha home? I need to talk to her."

The boy continued on to the car, but the woman stopped to look at me. "You just missed her." She brought her hand to her chest. "I'm her mother. She asked me to babysit today so she could go to an Amish wedding." She shook her head. "They hold 'em on Thursday mornings—can you believe such a thing?"

My heart beat painfully. "Why would she go to the wedding?" I asked dumbly.

"Miriam Coblenz is a friend of hers. They've known each other for years. Of course she'd be there for it." She pressed her lips together and scrunched up the side of her face. "Don't tell her I said so, but I think she wanted the opportunity to show off the new man in her life. She got herself all gussied up and I must admit, they're a handsome couple."

I turned and ran back to the car, not bothering to respond to the woman or even say goodbye. There wasn't any time. If

Brent didn't have enough reasons to go off the deep end before, he certainly did now.

I counted more than three dozen buggies lining the Coblenz's driveway. There were also a fair number of white vans parked and a dozen more cars in the yard. As I drove past the barns, I saw horses' heads sticking out from the tie stalls. The sounds of their nickering followed me up the gravel drive. A few boys in suspenders and wearing straw hats ran from the large metal building across the yard towards the house. On the front porch where I'd talked to Miriam, several women stood holding babies.

I parked with the other cars, lowered the windows and listened. The sound of a baby crying drifted on the breeze, along with the garbled sound of a man speaking in Pennsylvania Dutch. His voice was coming from the metal barnlike structure. The front half of the building was slightly shorter than the back half, giving me the impression that it was separated on the inside by a wall. The side facing the car had a line of garage doors that were all open. I could see the beards and black attire of dozens of men sitting on benches. When I lifted my sunglasses and squinted, I spotted colorful dresses beyond the men. It seemed as though the entire Amish community had squeezed onto benches in the building.

I inhaled and blew out slowly, carefully surveying the scene. Cows grazed on the other side of the fence and chickens pecked the ground between the cars. Every so often a small child would leave the building, breaking into a run when they neared the house. I relaxed a little and breathed easier. Most children would need a bathroom break during a three-hour church service.

When the sound of singing floated into the car, I sat perfectly still, listening. It was a loud, somber tune. No musical instruments accompanied the voices of the men and women, but I was impressed with the rhythmic changes of harmony between the sexes. It was a chorus that could rival any English church, but the song sounded more suitable for a funeral than a wedding.

When I clutched the door handle and stepped out, I felt the prickling sensation of silliness. I wasn't exactly sure what I was expecting before I arrived, but I now had little doubt now that I had gotten worked up over nothing. Miriam's wedding was in full swing, and as far as I could tell, everything was as it was supposed to be.

I was glad I hadn't called John and sounded a false alarm, potentially ruining the wedding for the bride and groom. But I didn't completely let my guard down as I forced myself to approach the building, walking a wide berth away from the garage doorways so that I wasn't as noticeable when I slipped in the furthest one. Just as I wanted, I was positioned at the back of the congregation.

I removed my sunglasses and let my eyes adjust to the dim interior of the room. The benches were set up on either side of an aisle. On the left, the men sat and on the right were the women. A couple of long benches were set up at the very back for the English guests. I followed the wall and sat on the first bench I came to. An older man smiled and pressed into his wife to make room for me. I smiled back, sitting down with a sense of relief that all eyes hadn't turned my way when

I'd entered the building. But several of the men had looked my way, and one ancient woman had been curious enough to even turn her head as I passed by.

Just as I'd thought, the building was separated into two rooms. A regular-sized doorway was open on the far wall and I caught a glimpse of long tables covered with white clothes and adorned with baskets filled with white flowers. Other than the flowers, I didn't see any other wedding decorations.

As my eyes searched the crowd, several thoughts flitted through my mind. The fact that the men and women were separated didn't entirely shock me as I'd seen previously how the sexes divided into two groups, but it still unnerved me seeing it play out in such an obvious way. But it was the depressive heaviness in the air that unsettled me the most. Everyone seemed so solemn and serious.

When I craned my neck, I saw Miriam and the groom sitting in the front row with their backs to the congregation. There was a couple sitting on either side of them. I could just barely make out her navy blue dress and the white apron that looked the same as the clothes I saw Amish women wearing every other day. The women beside her, who I assumed were her attendants, were dressed identically to her. How sad it was that Miriam couldn't look special on her wedding day.

I wasn't one of those women who'd spent a lot of time dreaming about my own wedding. Even with Daniel's proposal, I still hadn't giving it much thought. But I can say that I envisioned a brightly lit church, wildflower bouquets and a lot of smiling faces.

Samantha's blonde hair caught my eye at the end of the bench. She sat with a nice looking, middle-aged man. She

wore a floral patterned dress and he had on suit pants and
a button up shirt. I glanced down at my jeans and t-shirt and
chewed on my bottom lip. The man who sat next to me passed
me a program and I mouthed a thank you. The cover had a
picture of a bundle of white roses on it with the caption, "With
all humility and gentleness, with patience, bearing with one
another in love, eager to maintain the unity of the Spirit in
the bond of peace, Ephesians 4:2-3."

When I flipped it open, I was happy to see that it provided
an English translation. I skipped over the hymns and the sermon section, stopping at the marriage vows. Nothing too out
of the ordinary—both the husband and wife agreed that the
Lord had ordained the relationship, and to care for the other
if they became sick. The last vow was promising each other
that they would love and not separate from each other until
God separated them through death.

The congregation began singing again with the same dull
tempo of the first song I'd heard. I returned my gaze to the
program and read along.

> Now then, cheer up, you Church of God,
> Holy and pure these later times,
> You who are chosen unto a bridegroom
> Called Jesus Christ,
> Do prepare yourself for Him.
> Lay your adornments, for He comes soon,
> Therefore prepare the wedding garment,
> For He will certainly have the wedding,
> Now, allowing you to be parted from Him
> eternally.

When the song ended, a man with a long black beard peppered with gray began to speak. I guessed him to be this community's bishop. He rambled on in their language, but I did catch an occasional English word thrown in. The sermon went on, and on, and on. I slumped on the bench and my mind wandered. I found myself thinking about the bones in my butt I never even knew existed until this moment. I also wondered about Daniel. I'd made excuses why I couldn't return his phone calls and kept my text messages short. Having a conversation with him wouldn't help me focus. I needed to keep my emotions out of the investigation, and if I communicated with my fiancé, I wouldn't be able to do it.

The entire case was baffling. Brent Prowes appeared to be the most likely suspect. He had more than enough motive to kill his brother. He had the most to gain from Buddy's death and he had a crush on his sister-in-law. He didn't even try to hide his propensity to hold grudges, and he'd killed a dog, which is a marked trait for murderers. But all that wasn't enough to arrest him, and definitely not enough for a conviction.

There were also several Amish men being their usual secretive selves. Seth Hershberger and Lester Lapp had managed to conceal their identities of being on Buddy Prowes' work crew, and each of them had singled out Buddy's ex-wife, Samantha Prowes, as their prime suspect. And both of them had basically said in a typically Amish passive way that they thought their boss had it coming. Joshua Miller was an intriguing character, and he didn't bother to hide his dislike for Buddy, but I was willing to bet his greatest crime was arrogance. Then there was Danny Bach. His description and shortened name matched Daniel perfectly. And I'd caught him lying about his knowledge of Buddy and his time spent in Lancaster.

Could he really be involved in the murder?

The side of my temple throbbed, and I pressed my fingers to it and rubbed. I wished I'd never pursued the investigation with the marshals. Ignorance *was* bliss—Bobby was right. I was sworn to uphold the law and I was terrified that in doing so, I might destroy Daniel in the process. It had taken me a while to admit it, but I did love him—maybe even enough to shield him from the law if necessary. I'd listened to Bobby and my sister, Laura, but it would be up to me to make the impossible decision of what to do if I did discover that Daniel was guilty of something. Even though I'd taught him how to shoot a handgun, he'd hunted as a youth. It was plausible, since the murder weapon was a rifle, that he would have been able to shoot Buddy. And it wasn't farfetched that he could commit murder. Many otherwise good people had been pushed into taking someone's life for one reason or another. But I didn't for a minute believe he was capable of bludgeoning a body afterwards. Daniel didn't have that kind of anger inside of him. Whoever killed Buddy was a raging inferno of hatred.

When Miriam and Joseph Mast stood and faced each other, my eyes settled on the groom. The man who had stolen Miriam's heart after all these years was even taller than Daniel. He had a ruddy complexion and a sparse beard, but he was smiling at her in a way that made me like him instantly. Anyone paying attention could see the love he had for his bride.

The entire exchange of vows only lasted a few minutes and then another song began. The deep voices of the men filled the room and I gazed out one of the open doorways at the cows grazing in the pasture. Their tails flicked back and forth at flies. Occasionally a rooster crowed or a horse whinnied. I didn't bother to sing the song, instead using the program to fan myself. The air was becoming thick and warm with so many bodies squeezed into the room, and beads of sweat formed on the back of my neck.

When the women's sweet, high-pitched voices took over, I looked up. I couldn't see Miriam's face, but I imagined she was smiling. The rest of the crowd was reserved and seemed distant. When the song finally ended, the wedding party filed out of the room and into the adjoining room. Everyone was orderly and quiet. It was nothing like the joyful weddings I'd attended in the past. For my part, I usually found the occasions unpleasant. There was always an expectation of perfection that never became a reality, and then I had to talk to all those distant relatives or so-called friends and pretend to be interested in their lives. Most of the weddings I'd been to in the past, the couple were divorced within five years anyway. The statistics made me even more cynical.

I rose and stretched my back. I felt foolish for rushing over to the wedding as though something terrible was about to happen. Now I just wanted to get back to my car and be on my way. During the long sermon I'd had a lot of time to think. As much as a part of me wanted to know who killed Buddy Prowes, I would let the investigation go. But I did plan to talk to Daniel about everything when I got home. There could be no secrets between us—especially not a secret like this. If we were meant to be together, then he would say the right thing, and alleviate my fears. If not, then it was better I addressed it before we said our own wedding vows.

I squeezed through the crowd until sunshine hit my face. The sounds of quiet conversation and shuffling of feet fell away behind me as I put my sunglasses on and headed for the car. A hand on my shoulder stopped me and I spun around.

"You're staying for the dinner aren't you? It's the best part." Louise Schwartz stood there in a mint green dress with a beaming face.

I suddenly felt like the imposter I was. My stomach tightened and I took a breath. I just wanted to get out, but I didn't want to be rude to the poor girl. "I'm just going to the car to get the present," I lied.

She smiled back. "Oh, there's a tent—" she pointed to the side of the building "—set up for the gifts over there." She leaned in closer. "There's a table at the back of the reception room for the English guests. There will be a seat for you. You're going to love the roasted chicken." She glanced back at the building. "I'd better go. I'm one of Miriam's servers." Louise flashed another smile and turned on her heels, jogging away.

She was a nice girl, and even from here, the cooking smells reached me. I sniffed the air with longing as I watched Louise slip back into the crowd. A loud shriek drew my attention to a group of little girls running into the building. I recognized the smallest girl who'd waved at me at breakfast. She was at the front of the pack of girls. Their colorful dresses made the girls look like a moving bouquet of flowers.

The crowd was loosening up. Small groups of men and women stood around the metal building, the volume of their laughs and conversation rising. I grunted, but couldn't keep the grin from my mouth. This was as rowdy as the Amish seemed to get. Shaking my head, I turned away. I'd grab a greasy burger on the way out of town that I'd later regret. But I wanted to get home to have that conversation with Daniel. I'd waited long enough.

I heard the vibration in my purse and pulled out my cell phone. It was Daniel.

"Hey, what's going on?" I tried to sound upbeat, silently cursing my pounding heart.

"I'm just taking a leisurely drive. Where are you?" he asked.

"I'm still in Lancaster."

He snorted into the phone. "Todd already told me that."

"You called Todd?"

"What am I supposed to do when my fiancé won't return my calls?"

I glanced at the phone and saw five missed calls. "Sorry about that. I've been kind of busy here. You won't believe where I've just been."

"At the Coblenz wedding?" Daniel said innocently and the tone of his voice warmed my cheeks.

"How did you know that?"

He grunted. "A lady at the gas station told me all about the big wedding today. I figured since almost all of the Amish in the neighborhood would be there, so would you."

"You should have been a detective," I said dryly, but I was smiling. "Why are you here?"

"I missed you, and I figured if I didn't make the drive, I probably wouldn't see you for another day."

"It's just a day."

"I didn't want to wait."

My neck tingled at his words and I dipped my chin, smiling down at my booted feet. "How far out are you? I can give you directions."

"I know where the Coblenz farm is. I'm just pulling in now."

My head snapped towards the road and sure enough, Daniel's Jeep was making its way slowly up the gravel drive.

Another vehicle caught my eye. It was parked alongside the road. I took a few steps and stopped, frozen in place. *A gray pickup truck with dents.* My heart hammered so hard that it hurt. I shoved the phone back into my purse and started running towards the building.

A succession of gunshot blasts rang out. I counted ten and ran faster. The sounds jarred the peacefulness of the farm like mini explosions. I ran even faster. Women left their groups to rush to their husbands' sides with hands over their mouths, and several horses tied to a hitching rail bolted backwards until their ropes stretched tight.

I pulled my gun from its holster and waved people out of my way. "Police—clear a path!" I shouted.

The Amish were quick to respond, parting to make room for me to pass. I skidded into the shady interior of the room where only moments before everyone had watched Miriam and Joseph marry. My eyes immediately went to the doorway leading into the reception room. It was shut.

Caboom. Caboom. Caboom. I slammed sideways into the door, frantically turning the knob, but to no avail. It was locked.

"Is there another way in?" I searched the pale, disbelieving faces around me.

A young Amish man with just the beginning of a beard ran into the building at full tilt. "The side doors are barred!" He gasped, cupping his face with his hands.

Daniel flew up behind me and I caught my breath. "Call 911. We have an active shooter and hostages."

He drew his phone from his pocket and turned away without asking questions.

Pop. Pop. A different caliber gun was fired. Either there were two gunmen or the guy had multiple guns.

I scanned the crowd of people. No one was trying to flee. They were frozen there, shocked and staring at me. I recognized the bishop and hoped he was as clever as our bishop in Blood Rock. "Is there another way in?" I asked him.

He glanced around until his eyes fastened on a short, round man. "You know the barn—is there another entrance?"

The man pointed up. "There's a crawl space above us that is used for storage. It opens to the other side of the wall."

The bishop barked out orders in his language and the area was a sudden flurry of activity. Several men pulled up a table to the place where the chubby fellow directed. A few seconds later, another man climbed onto the table with a handsaw.

"They're on their way, but it must be fifteen miles to town from here," Daniel said.

"More like eighteen," the bishop countered.

Jerimiah appeared at my side. He grabbed my arm. "My wife and daughter are in there."

I looked into his watery eyes and my heart sank into my stomach. "I'm going to do my best to get them out."

"Why would someone do such a thing…" a woman trailed off, beginning to cry.

Another shot exploded on the other side of the wall and I met Daniel's wide eyes. He climbed onto the table and took the saw from the other man. He followed the seam between the plywood boards and forced his fingers in between them. With a grunting pull, he broke the board.

"There's enough room for me to go through." I tried to keep my voice from breaking as I climbed up beside Daniel with the bishop's help.

"It's not big enough for me to fit yet—you can't go in there alone," Daniel pleaded.

"Of course I can," I hissed. "It's my job." I holstered my gun. "Now lift me up."

Daniel's eyes darkened and I thought he was going to refuse. He swallowed, shook his head and put his arms around me. He was strong and I was small. With little effort, he hoisted me into the opening and pushed me though.

I was in the dark and assaulted with stifling, hot air. The ceiling was only inches above my head in a crawling position. The pink insulation prickled my skin and I fought the urge to sneeze as I made my way closer to the place where the ceiling rose. I heard muffled voices and sobbing.

I shuffled faster until I could finally rise up on my knees. I squeezed in between a stack of wood and an old, dusty harness, and peeked down into the room below.

I counted five people on the floor—two men and three women. One of the men was the groom and the other was Isaiah Coblenz. My hand went to my mouth when I saw Miriam's dead, staring eyes. Her head was turned at a grotesque angle and her arm stretched out to her husband, their fingers almost touching. A puddle of blood pooled around them.

I forced my feelings down and drew in a steady breath.

My eyes skimmed across the overturned tables and the once white table clothes now stained red. Broken bowls of food littered the floor, some still steaming. Many of the flower arrangements were untouched, lending to the surreal feel of the scene.

About eighty people were in the room, huddled in the corner. A line of men with black coats provided a barrier between Brent Prowes and the women. The children were kneeling in the center of the group. That's where most of the crying was coming from.

Brent had a hold of Samantha. He dragged her with one arm, waving a handgun around with the other. The semi-automatic was slung over his shoulder with a strap. He had a pouch on his belt that probably held more ammo.

I raised my gun to my eye and followed his movements. Todd was my sharp shooter and I relied on him to make the difficult shots. I had good aim, but I wasn't confident that I could make the shot on a man in motion with a struggling hostage.

"It's because of you my life is this way!" Brent shouted. "You did this—each and every one of you!"

His voice was desperate. He'd already killed at least five people, one of them a woman he had loved. There was no reasoning with him now. The only way to end this was for him to die.

But Seth Hershberger wasn't thinking like I was. I held my breath as he pulled away from his wife and took a few steps closer to the gunman.

Seth raised his hands. "Please Brent, don't do this. The children and women are scared. The Lord will forgive you— we all will forgive you."

"Forgive me?" Brent snarled. "Just like you forgave Buddy when he threw boards at you or when he struck his wife?" He shook Samantha and she clamped down on his arm with her mouth.

He hit her on the side of the head with his gun and her struggling lessened, but didn't stop entirely.

"I saw the note you wrote Buddy—and I understood what it meant. You wanted God to bless him for his actions. Why would you do such a thing?" Brent demanded.

Seth looked upwards and shut his eyes as though he was praying for help from a higher authority. When he looked back at Brent, he said in a voice scaling higher, "It's my people's way to forgive. We follow the way of grace in all things. It's what our Savior guides us to do."

Brent brought his arm up and aimed the gun at Seth. The room became dark and I focused on Brent's head, holding my hand steady. My finger began to press the trigger when Samantha's elbow came free and she swung it at Brent's face. He ducked, and his arm jerked, pressing his gun into her stomach.

"It's your fault—you fucking whore!" Spit flew from his mouth. "You're the one who told me if I did Buddy in, you'd be with me. But you were screwing another man that very same night!"

The revelation stalled my finger on the trigger as I listened.

"It's over. You've killed innocent people—for what? Revenge?" She lowered her voice and I strained to hear. "You stupid fool. I never wanted you."

Brent brought his face within inches of Samantha's. "You were able to fool everyone else, but you can't fool God. He knows what you did. You're going to rot in hell right beside me for killing Buddy."

He shoved Samantha at the Amish, stuffed the handgun into his pants and grabbed the rifle from his shoulder. Several voices gasped.

Amish men spread their arms wide and the women dropped to their children, shielding them the best they could.

I was too terrified to move.

Brent's rifle was in his hands and he aimed at the cowering crowd.

All I saw was Brent's head when my finger closed on the trigger.

20

My gun discharged with an explosion that momentarily deafened me. Brent fell forward and his rifle discharged several rounds into the floor. When he landed, the back of his head was blood and brain matter.

The wailing sound of sirens grew louder and the door below me splintered, breaking apart. Daniel, Jerimiah and the bishop fell into the room with what appeared to be a fence post. Martha was the first to run away from the group of hostages, dragging her daughter with her. She knelt down to Jerimiah and flung her arms around his neck before he even had the chance to get up.

Several men dropped to their knees beside their fallen people. I heard the bishop praying and several women sobbing. I couldn't breathe as my eyes searched the Amish crowd as they straightened up, dazed and slow. A woman clutched her arm and a man carried a little boy whose white shirt was stained with blood. As the group separated, I saw another woman on the ground, not moving.

Louise clutched the side of an elderly woman, but neither of them appeared injured, and I spotted the little girl from breakfast in her father's arms. She was crying and alive. I finally breathed.

Daniel looked up and met my gaze. I returned my gun to its holster and scooted to the edge of the storage space. I slid down the wall into his strong arms.

When I pressed my face into his chest, my eyes filled with tears, even though I fought to hold them in. Poor Miriam. After all the years of waiting, she finally married, and then she died, along with her husband, father and three other people. The senseless killings left my mind numb. A day of happiness had turned into a massacre, *and I couldn't stop it from happening.*

John and Toby were the first law enforcement through the door, followed by a sea of uniformed officers, some holding their guns out and others talking on their radios. Several pairs of paramedics were right behind them.

I sniffed, wiping the back of my hand across my eyes as I watched everyone doing their jobs.

"Are you all right?" John touched my arm.

I dared to look up, willing myself to bury the emotions deep inside of me. "I'm fine." I lifted my chin. "The bride and groom weren't so lucky."

"Was it our guy, Brent?" Toby asked, scanning the room.

I pointed to his body. "I took him out with a single shot before he opened up on the crowd. It might have been much worse."

"How did you know he'd come here?" John tilted his head, his eyes probing.

I leaned against Daniel. "I put myself in his shoes and followed my gut. If I was a killer and I knew all the people who had ever pissed me off were going to be in one room, this is where I would have been. Miriam's wedding signified the end of any possibility of him being with her. It was the final straw. Brent hated Isaiah Coblenz for taking his business and keeping his daughter away from him. He also hated Seth Hershberger for being kind to Buddy, even when Buddy had been so horrible to him. Brent couldn't understand the Amish philosophy of forgiveness." My eyes strayed across the room. Samantha was sitting on the ground, hugging her knees. Her date stood next to her, looking as stunned as everyone else. "And then there's Samantha Prowes. When I learned she was attending the wedding, I had the feeling something bad was going to happen."

John rubbed his chin. "How did you know Brent was Buddy's killer?"

"When Jerimiah told us about Brent beating the dog, I just knew. Classic psychology. Only really bad guys kill dogs or family pets for no good reason. But there were a couple pieces of the puzzle that didn't jive my theory. One was the note left in Buddy's car and the other was Samantha." I glanced between John and Toby. "Things were said in this room that answered those questions and put the final pieces of the puzzle into place." I nodded at Samantha. "You need to arrest her on conspiracy to commit murder on Buddy Prowes."

John's brows lifted. "Do we have enough evidence to convict her?"

"She's a lawyer, so who the hell knows for sure, but I can attest you have at least sixty adult witnesses in this room, plus me, who heard Brent accuse her of asking him to murder his brother. Her response to the accusation didn't help her. I think you have a closed case."

John's face brightened as he looked at Samantha. "Good work, Sheriff. I knew you'd be helpful on the case, but I never dreamed this instrumental in getting our man...and woman."

"And saving countless lives," Toby added.

"It's all part of the job." My eyes wandered over Miriam's body again.

A man in a suit knelt beside the body, being careful not to step in the blood. The puddle had spread, finding its way to a cluster of roses scattered across the floor. Their white petals soaked up the blood, turning red. I stared at the petals, unable to look away.

A uniformed man approached John. When he spoke, it sounded distant, almost dreamlike. "The media is already arriving and the sheriff is busy keeping the Amish from leaving. What should I do with them?"

"Rope off an area down by the road and tell the reporters to set up there. I don't want any of them harassing the families."

John nudged me. I was almost too numb to feel his touch.

"I'm afraid you won't be able to head back to Blood Rock for a few days. This is going to be a nightmare to get sorted out." I raised my gaze to his and he frowned at me. His eyes flicked to the broken door. "Why don't you get some fresh air—we'll do a formal interview later."

I freed my gun from its holster and handed it to him. "I'm sure you're going to need it for the forensics."

John's lips pressed together and he took the gun.

The smell of death and gun powder was strong in the air and I couldn't wait to get out of the building. I turned to leave when Daniel's hand folded around mine, stopping me.

I looked into his eyes and my heart sank.

"I think there's a piece of the puzzle you haven't figured out yet." He took a deep breath. "That's one of the reasons I came to Lancaster—to talk to you about it."

Toby's brows shot up, and John's eyes popped wider as he stared at Daniel. He'd just made the connection with Danny Bach.

"Not now, Daniel. It isn't the time." I pleaded at John with my eyes.

John's lips curved to the side and he looked at me with a sharp, calculating gaze. Then his expression relaxed. "We have a lot on our plate at the moment. We'll catch up with you soon, Daniel. You need to comfort Serenity right now. She needs you."

Toby winked at me before he followed John into the crowd of officers.

"I'm sorry I wasn't truthful with you," Daniel said in a soft voice.

I disengaged my hand and headed for the door.

When I stepped out into the sunlight, I dropped my head back and closed my eyes.

"Thank you."

I opened my eyes to see Martha standing in front of me. Her daughter was under her arm, staring at the ground, Jerimiah a few steps behind her.

"Jerimiah told me how you risked your life to go into crawl space to save us." She reached out, took my hand and squeezed it. "You're an angel." Her eyes watered and she covered her mouth, hurrying away. Jerimiah dipped his hat and mouthed a thank you before he caught up to his wife and daughter.

Blinking cruisers and ambulances crowded the driveway. I looked down to the road to where the gray pickup was still parked. Cows grazed beyond the frenzy of activity and chickens flapped their wings to escape being stepped on.

The sky was the deepest blue and little white puffs of clouds floated above. I lifted my face into the warm breeze.

"It seems like the most terrible things tend to happen on the prettiest days," I said out loud, but I meant to only think it. I looked up at Daniel and shielded my eyes from the sun. "Will the people here actually forgive Brent for what he did?"

"The way of grace is the Amish way. Healing from a tragedy like this can only come from forgiveness."

I shook my head. "I could never forgive him. Lives were taken today, stolen away from innocent people—you can't get over something like this."

"I didn't say they'd get over it. This day will haunt their dreams forever. But they're a resilient people. They will move on…and they will forgive."

Maybe I wasn't so different from Brent after all.

I knew I would definitely hold a grudge.

21

Daniel pulled off the road and parked the Jeep. No cars were in Samantha's driveway, and the house looked empty. I wondered about her son and what would happen to him if she served prison time. He'd probably end up being raised by his grandmother with some visitation from his biological father. It was a tough situation for the kid to be in, but living with a mother who'd arranged her first husband's murder wasn't any better. A woman like that would be paranoid as hell. And that wouldn't make for good mothering or a pleasant upbringing.

"Why did you bring me here?" I glanced at Daniel, who was staring at the woods behind the house.

He raised his chin in the direction of the trees. "That's where Buddy was shot."

I followed his gaze, but didn't say anything.

"I was here that night—in the house." He drew in a deep, unsteady breath and I turned to stare at him. "Samantha and I were *involved* at the time. It had only been going on for a few weeks before Buddy's murder, and ended about a week after."

My mouth was dry and my lips frozen, but I forced myself to speak. "Why didn't you tell me about this when I first mentioned the case to you, right after the marshals showed up?"

He swallowed, looking straight ahead and I didn't blink. "I was afraid to say anything." He glanced my way. "From the very beginning, you didn't trust me. It took so long for you to let me in—for you to accept my love. When I asked you to marry me, I wasn't sure you'd even say yes." He ran his hand through his hair with a tug. "The last thing I wanted to do was bring up my past, my bachelor days, when I used to flit from one girl to the next, like a lost soul."

His words settled in my mind and my eyes narrowed. "A man was murdered here, while you were screwing his ex-wife. That's a hell of lot more important than hurting my feelings." He opened his mouth and I thrust my hand into the air. "You changed your name and were faking your identity. You had Mervin and Seth cover for you—probably even Jerimiah."

"I already told you when I left Blood Rock I was fighting my own demons. Those first few years were incredibly tough on me. I went from having no freedom, to having too much, and then I'd lost my family—my parents and my siblings were strangers to me." When my eyes remained hard, he added, "I'm not trying to make excuses. I just want you to understand where I was at that point in my life. I wasn't in a good state of mind in those days."

"Why did you go to Lancaster if you had left the Amish?"

"The transition to the outside world was too much for me. I missed the familiarity of culture and language. I didn't want to go back to being Amish, but I missed being around the Amish, if that makes any sense. Since I couldn't return to

Blood Rock, I picked a distant community where no one knew me, except two of my closest friends. They kept my secret and everyone there thought I was just another English young man looking for work. Jerimiah had no idea of the truth."

I inhaled and blew out slowly. As much as I wanted to be angry with Daniel, I couldn't muster a strong enough emotion. I was still dazed from the wedding massacre. There was a painful chill of solitude around me that I couldn't shake, making me feel as though I was removed from my body, staring down at it from afar. My jealousy over a fling Daniel had fifteen years ago was trivial in comparison to what had happened today.

I inhaled, trying to wake myself from the nightmare my mind couldn't escape. "We've been together for a while now, and we're engaged. Were you planning to keep this part of your life secret from me forever? Because I don't think skeletons in the closet make for a healthy marriage."

"I agree. They don't." He cupped his chin and glanced back at me and then away again. "This will sound terrible, but I'm putting all my cards on the table. I was planning to tell you everything sometime after our wedding. I wasn't going to do anything to jeopardize you becoming my wife." When my mouth dropped open, he came closer. "You're not like any woman I've been with before, Serenity. Everything is so damn black and white with you. I was sure you'd leave me if you found out about my affair with a woman whose husband was murdered and the case never solved."

"You were wrong. I wouldn't have held that against you— as long as you were up front with me about it. You should have trusted me."

"There is something else," he said quietly.

Sunshine was pouring in the windows, heating my face. I closed my eyes and lifted my face to it, afraid of what he was going to say.

There was a moment of silence in the cab and then he spoke up. "Samantha had hinted around that she wanted me to do something about Buddy." I turned to him and he hurriedly went on, "I mentioned it to Mervin and Seth and they warned me to get away from her, but I was young, stupid and lonely. She played me like a fiddle. She insisted I come over that night and when she brought up Buddy, we argued. I wanted no part in what she was talking about, and I was going to leave, but she stopped me."

"Did you see Buddy that night?" I asked, holding my breath.

He nodded. "Through the window, and I heard him. He was sneaking around the house, spying on Samantha. She suspected he was out there and she grabbed her shotgun and went out on the porch. I would've gone with her, but she insisted I stay in the house. She said if Buddy saw me there, he'd kill me for sure. It was a stormy night and I distinctly remember how I strained to hear their voices through the claps of thunder. My pickup truck was parked out front, so he already knew she wasn't alone. They yelled back and forth at each other for a couple of minutes and she threatened to shoot him, and then he left. Maybe twenty minutes or so later, we heard the gun blast. When daylight broke, we followed the path and found Buddy's body."

"You aren't mentioned on any of the reports—"

"No, I wouldn't be," he interrupted. "Samantha insisted I leave and never come back. She said if I stuck around, I'd probably be charged with the crime since I'd been there with her that night." He chuckled darkly, shaking his head. "At first I thought she was protecting me. Later I realized she was only taking care of herself. If the cops had talked to me, I might have told them about how she'd propositioned me to kill Buddy."

"You couldn't have been that stupid." My eyes bulged as I stared at the side of his face.

"I was scared. I didn't know anything about the English legal system back then. And I was alone, with only the guidance of a couple of Amish boys. Seeing Buddy lying there, nearly decapitated, I kind of lost it." He grunted and finally looked over. "Yeah, I ran. I ran away and never came back."

"Who did you think killed him?" I asked.

"Samantha was with me, so I knew she didn't pull the trigger, but she was a pretty woman. I figured she had found another guy to do her dirty work. I never dreamed it was her brother-in-law though. Brent was a little backward, but not a killer."

"He killed the dog."

"At the time it was disturbing, but I didn't make the connection that he had it in him to do the same thing to his brother. After all these years, I still don't understand why Samantha wanted Buddy dead so badly."

"Because she was very ambitious and Buddy stood in the way of achieving her goals. He wouldn't leave her alone—and that made finding another man to care for her impossible. She was probably planning to hook up with Brent after he inherited the building business, but when it went under, she changed her mind and married her second husband instead. That guy worked at a factory and brought in a decent paycheck. Not long after he was laid off, she filed for divorce again, only he was the type of person who backed off and left

Samantha alone, even though they shared a child together. At that point, she decided to make it on her own and got her degree and became a lawyer. But I wouldn't be surprised if the guy she's with now doesn't have money in the bank. She's just that type of gal."

"Where do we go from here?" Daniel looked at me.

"You have to tell the marshals the entire story. There's a good chance Samantha will spill the beans at some point that you were with her the night of the murder. You don't want that coming back to bite you in the butt."

"All right, I'll do it. But what about us—do we still have a chance?"

I wanted to avoid the question, but I couldn't. Maybe if I hadn't given him such a hard time about our relationship, he would have felt comfortable talking to me sooner about Samantha and Buddy. In a way, I'd helped to create the situation we were in. I didn't want to lose Daniel—even though a part of me still buried beneath the lifelessness I felt now was really pissed he'd kept his involvement with Samantha and Buddy a secret from me.

But then my thoughts flashed to that afternoon. I remembered Miriam's hand outstretched, almost touching her new husband's hand while they lay next to each other—dead. *How tragic their story had ended.* I wouldn't take Daniel or our love for granted. I pushed my hand into his and he eagerly took it and squeezed.

Panic tightened my throat, but I forced myself to speak. "When I told you I loved you, I meant it. Everyone has bumps along the road, this is just a really big one for us. You're going to have to give me some time. But I think we'll be okay."

"Are you keeping the ring on?" he asked cautiously.

I glanced down and it sparkled in the sunlight. It had felt so awkward wearing it at first, but sometime in the last couple of weeks I'd gotten used to it.

I wiggled my finger. "Isn't it part of the whole being engaged thing?"

Daniel laughed and pulled me against him. When his mouth opened over mine, I sighed and kissed him back as though it was our last kiss. Tingling sensations spread through my body, chasing some of the numbness away.

I hardly knew Miriam, but I'd never forget the short time I'd spent with her, rocking on the front porch and sharing her secrets or the sight of her pale, dead face.

Life was too damn short. I was going to do my best not to waste a single moment of mine.

22

Toby peeked out and flicked his finger for me to enter the interrogation room. I practically leaped from the chair and burst through the door.

The room was small and the walls were covered with outdated paneling, but otherwise it wasn't much different from the one we had in Blood Rock. John sat across the table from Daniel. He set his pen down, closed the file folder and pushed it to the side. The recorder was turned off. I found it difficult to breathe as I sat in the chair beside Daniel.

John looked up and offered a small smile. "If your fiancé had come forward all those years ago, Jim wouldn't have gone to his grave wondering who killed Buddy Prowes."

I pursed my lips. "I'm not so sure about that. Daniel didn't have any idea it was Brent—he just suspected Samantha had talked someone into taking out her ex."

"I've always thought it was odd how when the truth comes to light, everybody is either completely shocked or they suspected it all along. In Buddy's case, Jim wrote notes of his suspicions about her involvement in the murder, but he never found anyone to link her to it. Brent didn't leave any evidence behind and no one had reason to think he was out to get his brother because his romantic relationship with Samantha was hidden from the world. She used him to get what she wanted—and he fell for it, hook, line and sinker."

"Brent Prowes was a psychopath." I snorted. "All he needed was a little nudging from his sister-in-law."

"That may be so, but now we have the word of a reputable lawyer in town against a dead man who murdered six people and wounded several others at an Amish wedding." He leaned back and groaned. "Without Daniel's testimony, we have nothing concrete to convict her."

I crossed my arms on the table, lifting my chin at Daniel. "Isn't his testimony enough? She practically asked him to kill her husband."

"That's not how it happened." Daniel spoke up. He met my stare. "She hinted at it, but never came right out and asked me to." He motioned with his hands. "She made me uncomfortable for sure, but that's it."

John shook his head. "Now that Buddy's killer is dead, I don't have reason to press any charges on Daniel for not coming forward with evidence earlier." He looked grim. "But I also don't have enough evidence to press charges against Samantha. Unfortunately, I think we're going to have to let her go."

Thoughts swirled around in my head and none of them were nice. I couldn't swear that my obsessive desire to put Samantha behind bars didn't have to do with the fact that she had been Daniel's lover at one time. But the idea that her cajoling Brent to murder his brother had somehow led to the wedding massacre and Miriam's death fifteen years later was the main reason I wanted her held accountable. She set into motion a string of events that had taken many years to play out, but they had played out in the most horrible way possible. I remembered how Samantha had been careful with her responses to Brent, even though people were dead at her feet, and she was being held in a vice grip with a gun against her stomach. She was a calculating bitch—and I wasn't going to let her get away with it.

I blinked and gazed at John. He inclined his head, waiting. "What if another man came forward—someone else who Samantha had solicited to take Buddy out?"

"Does such a person exist?" John's brows shot up as his looked between me and Daniel.

I turned to Daniel. "Do you know anyone else she was friendly with back then?" When he began to lift his shoulders in a shrug, I leaned in closer. "Think, Daniel. Think hard on this. You didn't know she was messing around with Brent either, but she was. If she was desperate enough, she very well might have flirted with another man and said something to him that, along with your testimony, would incriminate her."

Daniel dropped his head back and pressed his hands into his temples. His eyes were tightly closed. John's were wide open and bright with rising excitement.

After a long pause, he straightened back up and looked me in the eye. "There is one person who you might want to talk to—Joshua Miller."

23

Approaching the farmhouse, I noticed there was a lot less bustle in the Miller driveway than when I'd been here a few days ago. Rays of sunshine burned off the morning mist that hung over the pastures, and a flock of chickens pecked the ground beside the barn. I spotted pigs in the corral and a gray tabby walking along the top rail of the enclosure. Several kids moved about in the barnyard doing their chores, reminding me of Rowan Schwartz's offspring. Amish children got up early, even on Saturdays.

My thoughts strayed to Brent's three children and how they'd sat on the couch, pretending to watch television as their eyes darted to me and their mother whispering in the doorway. I'd seen the shock in her eyes when I'd first told her about what her ex-boyfriend and the father of her kids had done before I'd shot him dead. Her eyes had become misty, but she did not cry. Shock was like that. Sometimes it took a while for the full impact of what had happened to really sink in. Tonya was a tough lady—she'd survive. But from my own experiences, I was sure she'd forever question herself, wondering what she might have done differently to save him and the Amish people who'd died.

I gave my head a little shake and glanced over at Toby, who was riding shotgun. His cowboy hat was pulled down, concealing his face. He appeared to be napping. With the wedding massacre bringing national attention, John couldn't get away from his obligations in Lancaster, so he'd sent Toby with me to talk to Joshua. We'd left in the middle of the night, grabbed some coffee and only stopped for bathroom breaks. I yawned, but got a jolt of adrenaline when I saw Joshua step out the front door of his new house.

I pulled over and shut off the engine, smacking Toby's arm. "Wake up. It's show time."

Toby pushed his hat back and stretched. He popped his neck and took a sip of his cold coffee. I smiled when he grimaced.

"Are you always so damn perky in the morning?" He scrunched up his face.

"Since I haven't slept, it doesn't really make a difference what time it is. You're the first person to ever call me perky though."

"Hmm." Toby looked around. "So the guy's home?"

I lifted my chin towards the house. "He's having morning coffee and surveying his new empire. If you're nice, he'll probably offer you a cup." I snorted. "It's a thing with the Amish. They're usually hospitable, even when they're being questioned."

"You seem to have a love-hate relationship with them," Toby said.

My eyes drifted to the little girl carrying a bucket from the barn. Water sloshed out onto her green dress, but she kept walking until she reached the pig corral where there was a gap just wide enough for her to pour the water in for the pigs without having to open the gate.

"They're hard working people and good neighbors. Some have given me fits with their secretive ways, but others have been straightforward. The women are amazing cooks and you've got to commend them on their strong sense of faith. But I've come to learn that they have their demons just like everyone else. And unfortunately, because of their strict society, they tend to sweep the bad things under the rug." I turned to face him. "When they do have a problem, they try to solve it themselves, which usually doesn't work out very well."

"I'd say there's never a dull moment around here." Toby chuckled.

"You've got that right." I opened the door and looked back over my shoulder. "I'll be shocked if we get anything out of this guy. I already have him pegged as one of the more secretive ones."

"But he did give you the information about Jerimiah Suggs."

"True, but I think he had his own motives for doing so."

"And what would that be?"

"To bury his own demons."

We walked up to the porch. Joshua's brow lifted when he saw us.

"It's mighty early for a visit from the law." He tilted his head. "Would you like coffee?"

Toby smiled broadly and winked at me. "Yes, sir. That would be most welcome."

"Make mine black," I said.

Joshua opened the screen door and called into the house. A moment later, Toby and I were sitting on a bench, holding steaming cups in our hands and the Amish man was leaning against the porch railing. Occasionally a cow bellowed, but otherwise it was quiet.

I looked up at the tall man staring at me. "Have you heard news from Lancaster?"

Joshua pursed his lips and shook his head. "I've been so busy getting moved in, I haven't had time to socialize with anyone in this community, let alone my old one." He smirked and twirled the end of his beard between his fingers. "Since we don't have televisions, computers and cell phones, we get our news later than everyone else."

Daniel had already verified that the community that Joshua had moved from wasn't the same one where Brent went on his killing spree. But still, I knew how the Amish were all interconnected through marriages and business. I took a quick breath and said softly, "There was a tragedy at Miriam Coblenz's wedding." His eyes widened in recognition and I continued, "Brent Prowes went to the wedding and shot and killed six people, including the bride and groom, and the bride's father." I pulled my small notebook from my pocket and handed it to him. "Here's the list of names of the deceased."

Joshua read quickly and smoothed his hand down his beard. When he looked up, his face was a shade whiter. "How could this happen?"

"It turns out Brent Prowes killed his brother fifteen years ago. Somehow he managed to stay partially sound all these years, but he snapped on Thursday. The past came back to haunt him."

"Was he…arrested?" Joshua asked in a wavering voice.

"He's dead. I shot him."

His eyes widened even more, but he didn't say anything for a few long seconds. When he did recover, his voice was once again steady. "Why did you come here to tell me the news personally?"

I set my cup down on the bench and leaned forward, resting my arms on my knees. "Because I need your help. Brent didn't murder Buddy on his own behalf—he was asked to do so by a pretty young woman who he had a crush on." I searched his gray eyes, looking for a spark of something familiar. "She's going to get away with her part in the scheming unless someone else comes forward and testifies that she had approached him about killing her husband."

Joshua drew in a sharp breath. "I don't know what you're talking about."

I felt my face flush, but I held my irritation in and drew in a long breath. "You're lying. Do you remember Danny Bach? He used to Amish. He lives here in Blood Rock and also happens to be my fiancé." I paused, letting Joshua digest the information before I went on. "He was also involved with Samantha Prowes. He remembered seeing you leave her house one evening. It left a strong impression on him since he recalled you being an exceptionally by-the-book kind of Amish guy. The kind who judged his peers harshly when they disobeyed the rules."

Shock, anger and sadness passed over his face before he looked resignedly back at me. "Unlike the other boys, I always loved being Amish. Farming and working with the horses and the livestock is in my blood. I understood the need for strict rules at an early age and wasn't resentful of them. All I wanted to do was marry, raise a family and have my own farm." His eyes became distant and his face twisted. "But I was tempted. At the moment when I should have been the strongest, I was weak—and it's haunted me all these years."

Toby spoke up. "You must have been nineteen or twenty— you're allowed a mistake or two at that age."

Joshua shook his head roughly. "No. I was courting Miranda at the time, and I betrayed her trust."

The same little girl who I'd seen giving water to the pigs trotted up to the porch. She spoke to her dad in their language and he barked out a response that made the girl sprint away back towards the barn. He bent down and pressed his hands into his face.

"She's gone now, and I never got the chance to ask her forgiveness." He pointed at the retreating girl. "Nora's a miniature version of her mother."

I found it difficult to breathe. The man hadn't recovered from the death of his wife, and here I was pressing a knife into those still stinging wounds. But I needed Joshua's cooperation to put Samantha behind bars.

I lowered my voice. "I know this is difficult, and I don't mean to bring up bad memories, but now's your chance to finally make things right with Miranda. Even if she's not here in person, I'm sure she'd want you to come clean—to get it off your chest once and for all. I think she'd want Samantha Prowes to pay for her sins." Joshua looked up slowly with wet eyes and I asked, "Did you have a romantic relationship with Samantha?"

He nodded slowly.

"Did she ever ask you to kill Buddy?"

"Yes, she did." He hurriedly added, "But I never did anything to the man. That's what made me leave her for good. I saw her for what she really was and I hated myself for becoming involved with her in the first place." He hung his head. "She was an evil woman."

"Would you be willing to come into town with us and give a formal statement about what you just told me, and to testify in court later if you're asked?" I asked.

"This move is a new beginning for my family. I want to start over fresh, bury the bad memories." He gazed down the driveway and then returned his eyes to me. "Admitting that I was carrying on with an English woman while I was courting Miranda will tarnish my image here…but I think you're right about Miranda. She never liked the way Samantha flirted with me. She'd want me to tell the truth. "I'll go with you to give the statement, but I'm not sure about testifying in court. Our people don't usually get involved with English law."

It was a good start. And his written statement should be enough to get a grand jury indictment. I looked over at Toby and his grin told me he was satisfied with the outcome, at least for now.

I stood up and Joshua held up his hands. "I can't go right now. I'm meeting with a possible renter for the place down by the road." He pointed at the white farmhouse we'd passed when we'd turned into the driveway.

"That's yours too?"

"It came with the purchase. I advertised it last week and had an immediate reply from someone in Indianapolis. I guess he wants to get away from city life for a while. His name is CJ West. It shouldn't take too long to talk to the man."

A black car pulling a small trailer behind it came slowly up the driveway. A cloud of dust billowed around it from the gravel and I squinted to see it better. A tickling of anticipation ran up my spine as I stared at the car making its way closer.

CJ West. I knew that name.

The car parked beside mine, and I caught Toby's questioning brow when the door opened. I ignored his look and followed Joshua down the steps.

A slender woman stepped out of the car and slammed the door behind her. She looked out of place with her short black jacket and knee high black boots. She had bouncy brown curls down to her shoulders and a round face. Her blue eyes were wide spaced and her nose small and upturned. She looked around the barnyard with a slight smile. She was too distracted by the Amish man looming over her to recognize me.

She thrust her hand out. "Are you Joshua Miller?"

Joshua was flustered and ignored her hand all together. "I am. Who are you?"

"CJ West. I'm here about renting the house."

"There's some kind of mistake. I spoke to a man…"

CJ laughed, and the sound of it made the air warmer. "That was my brother who called you on my behalf." Her delicate brows rose. "Since you already cashed the deposit check, I hope there isn't any problem with me renting the place?"

Joshua looked back at me and Toby, begging for some kind of rescue, but he definitely wasn't getting it from me. I removed my sunglasses. "Camille Josephine West—is that really you?"

CJ's eyes bulged. "Oh my God! Serenity, what are you doing here?" She bounced forward and pinned me in a tight hug.

The bewildered expression on Joshua's face was priceless. I quickly disengaged from CJ and said, "In Indy, CJ worked as a paralegal in the justice department. She's also my former partner's girlfriend."

"*Was* his girlfriend," she said tightly.

My heart sank into my stomach. Ryan and CJ were one of those perfect couples that everyone else envied. I'd expected them to get married, have a boatload of kids and live happily ever after.

Nothing ever worked out like it was supposed to.

"I'm sorry, CJ. I didn't know."

She shrugged and worked hard to smile back at me. "It's been a difficult time." She took a short breath and changed the subject. "Is this the town you're sheriff in?" When I nodded, she said, "Ryan mentioned it a while back, but I never thought to call you. My life has been a bit of a mess lately. I'm hoping this move will help me get it back in order."

"This is my county. I'm off duty at the moment. What are you planning to do for a living here?" I spread my arms wide.

"For a change, I'm following my dreams and going back to painting."

"You're an artist?" Joshua interrupted.

"An aspiring one." She looked around. "If the beauty of the country doesn't light a fire with my creative juices, nothing will."

I could count on one hand the number of girlfriends I'd had in my entire life, and CJ would have been on the list. She was honest and silly and loyal to a fault. The idea that she was moving into town brightened my day considerably.

"I'm sorry, but I can't rent you the house," Joshua said, and all our eyes turned to him.

"Why not?" I demanded.

"It wouldn't be appropriate for me to have an unmarried woman living on my property," Joshua replied weakly. "The church wouldn't allow it."

CJ's face deflated and her shoulders slumped. But I wasn't ready to give in that easily. This was twenty-first century America and not the middle ages, after all.

"Since this was a misunderstanding, I'm sure Bishop Esch will make an exception to the rule, at least temporarily." I motioned to the trailer behind CJ's car. "I mean, what are you going to do, put her out on the street? You accepted her deposit money." I narrowed my gaze on him. "There are laws, you know."

Joshua stepped back and his mouth dropped open, but CJ stopped him by touching his arm. His gaze left me for her, and then her hand. His mouth curled back as if it were the mouth of a venomous snake.

"Please, Mr. Miller. I won't bother you at all. I promise. I really need peace and solitude in my life right now and the opportunity to live out here in the country was an answer to a prayer. Please let me stay."

CJ held his gaze with pleading eyes. She was a very pretty woman and also a damsel in distress. I watched Joshua to see if she was affecting him. The air changed, sparking with sudden, palpable energy and I realized that she *had* made an impact.

He disengaged his arm, but not in a harsh way, and touched his beard. "For the time being you can stay. But I can't make any long-term promises until I meet with the bishop and the ministers."

CJ's smile was radiant. "Oh, thank you, Mr. Miller. You won't regret this decision."

He let out a breath. "We'll see about that." He turned to me and Toby. "I'll let her into the house and give her the key, and then I'll be able to go into town with you."

"Toby will conduct the interview." I told him and glanced at CJ. "How about lunch at the best diner in town?"

"Sounds perfect." CJ beamed.

Joshua climbed into CJ's car. She backed up and they headed back down the driveway.

"That's the ingredients for trouble, if you ask me," Toby said.

"No one was asking," I replied.

But inwardly, I agreed wholeheartedly.

24

"What's going on with you?" I folded my arms over the table in Nancy's Diner and studied CJ's face.

She finished chewing her forkful of salad and pushed the plate away, mimicking my gesture. "Ryan cheated on me." When my mouth opened, she held up her hand and went on, "I know it's hard to believe. I was in denial for a while." Her voice dropped. "He was fooling around with Andrea Knott, the secretary at the precinct."

I searched my memories until I recalled the short brunette, who had a hard face and never smiled. I shook my head, angry at Ryan, and men in general.

"What the hell was wrong with him?" I growled.

CJ forced a smile, but her eyes glistened with emotion. "He said it was because I was pushing him to get married and he wasn't ready." She sat back. "Maybe it *was* me. I was pretty insecure about our relationship from the beginning."

I shook my head vigorously. "Don't you dare say that! You were dating for what, two years? That's enough time for a guy in his thirties to be ready for commitment. The affair was just an excuse. Someone like that will never be ready. Pressuring him was the right call. At least you know what he's really all about and this didn't happen after you had a mortgage and two kids."

"That would really have sucked." She pouted and then a reluctant grin appeared on her mouth. "It's good to see you again, Serenity. You're always so confident. I wish I was more like you."

CJ looked down at the table, devoid of personality. I remembered her as a vivacious and happy person—and kind too. She was the type of girlfriend who noticed when you were down and would bake brownies or tell you dirty jokes to cheer you up. Looking at my old friend now, I wanted to drive to Indianapolis and strangle Ryan myself. *How could he do this to her?* If he wasn't happy in the relationship, he should have just told her, and they both could have moved on without the humiliation and pain he'd caused her.

I took a sip of my cola and waited for her to glance up. When she did, I said, "I always envied your spunkiness. Nothing seemed to bring you down. You can't let this eat away at you." The sky outside brightened with the passing cloud and I nodded out the window. "One door closes, another opens. The breakup is an opportunity for you to start a new chapter of your life." I threw up my hands. "But here? I don't get it."

She laughed and for the first time since we'd sat down in the booth, I saw the mischievous twinkle in her eye that I was accustomed to. "It can't be all that bad—you're a resident."

I shrugged lamely. "I grew up in Blood Rock. My sister and her family are here—I know people." I tilted my head. "And unlike you, I'm anti-social."

CJ pursed her lips. "I had to get away. After I found out about Andrea, I confronted Ryan and for a while he denied it. I was stupid, wanting to believe him. When I came home one night after work and discovered the used condom in the trash can, I kicked him out of the apartment we shared. Not long after, he started seeing a new woman—a college student in her early twenties. Every so often I'd see them around town together, and even though I didn't want him back, I still couldn't stand seeing him all happy and smiling with her."

"What a sick jerk." I grunted and crumpled up the nearest napkin, squeezing it tightly and imagining it was Ryan's skull. "He'll do the same thing to her someday. Mark my words."

"Why would he? She's young and beautiful, and she's probably not bothering him for a ring."

Nancy popped her head over and paused beside the booth. "You ladies ready for dessert?"

"I think I'll pass," CJ said.

"Nonsense. A piece of Nancy's triple chocolate cake is just what you need." I held up two fingers. "Make it two—and put the entire order on my tab."

"Sure thing, honey." Nancy eyed CJ with raised brows before she went on her way.

"Is there a reason *you* need chocolate cake?" CJ flashed me a knowing look after her gaze paused on my engagement ring.

I exhaled. It had been a while since I talked to a girlfriend about my problems. I usually kept my problems to myself. If things were really bad, I'd breakdown and let Laura in, and sometimes Todd or Bobby. I talked to Daniel, but I couldn't help being a bit guarded around him. I considered Katherine and Rebecca to be friends, but the former was still recovering from her oldest son's death and the latter was Daniel's sister.

Both were also Amish, so their outlook on life didn't usually match my own. Having another female around who was close to my age and dealing with her own relationship issues might be just what I needed.

"So you noticed." I lifted my finger and looked at the glittering diamond.

"Who could miss it?" She reached over and touched my finger, craning her neck for a better look. "It's beautiful." She looked up. "Who's the lucky guy?"

I pulled my hand back and tucked it into my lap. "His name is Daniel Bachman. He has his own building business in town." I glanced around and lowered my voice. "He used to be Amish."

I appreciated her startled expression. I used to feel the same way.

"How is that going?" she managed to say.

"He's a great guy, but like everyone else, he has some issues. It's traumatic to leave your culture—your friends and family. He can be very secretive because of his upbringing and that's been a problem sometimes."

"You don't seem overjoyed about the engagement," she said carefully.

I chewed on my lip and sighed. "I have mixed emotions. I just got off an investigation involving a cold case murder. Daniel lied about it. I understand his reasons, but I can't stop wondering if his Amish background is going to cause us problems in the future. And that's not something that can be changed."

"This might sound ridiculous coming from me right now, but you shouldn't look too far into the future. If we all did that, no one would ever get married. If you love him, give him a chance." She popped another french fry into her mouth. "If it involved a roving eye, I'd insist you run for the hills. But this is different, and people can change. I think."

Her advice made my spirits rise. She was saying the same thing I'd been telling myself the entire drive back to Blood Rock. Daniel deserved a chance. But even though I could use my own therapy, I saw CJ's downcast eyes and heard her soft sigh. As hard as it was to believe, she needed help more than I did at the moment.

"Aren't you a little intimidated about living on an Amish farm in the middle of nowhere?" I asked, trying to keep her engaged, but also out of curiosity.

Her eyes drifted out the window. "It's going to be strange, that's for sure, but I'm looking forward to some quiet time painting." When her eyes returned, there was a spark that hadn't been there before. "Joshua Miller seems like a nice man." Her cheeks reddened and she dropped her voice. "He's good looking too."

My heart rate sped up when I saw CJ working to keep the smile from her face. It was healthy for CJ to get back in the game, but not with an Amish guy.

"I noticed some chemistry between the two of you when you met, but honestly, I wouldn't be a friend if I didn't warn you to avoid that temptation."

"Would it be so bad?" she asked with arched brows.

"He's Amish—they aren't allowed to date an outsider."

She giggled. "Maybe I wasn't talking about dating."

I rubbed my face. "That would be even worse." I recalled Joshua's tall frame and smoky eyes. He was eye candy, but his stubborn, arrogant personality made him a lot less appealing in my book.

"I don't know much about him," I admitted.

I spotted Elayne Weaver come through the door. She was wearing a pink, satiny blouse, short black skirt and four inch heels. No one would believe the assistant DA used to be Amish. I still had a difficult time wrapping my mind around it sometimes. She caught my eye and waved. I didn't have to motion her over—she was already on her way.

"I saw on the news about the wedding in Lancaster." Her face paled and she swallowed. "I can't even imagine how awful it was." She put her hand over mine. "It's a good thing you were there."

I slid over in the booth and Elayne took the unspoken invitation to sit down. I cleared my throat. "How do you know that? The feds and marshals are keeping the details under wraps for the time being. I'm supposed to return to Lancaster tomorrow, and then the entire world will know I was the one who brought down the shooter."

"It was *you* who stopped that guy?" CJ exclaimed.

I raised my hand and shot a warning look at her. "Shh. I have one more day of peace and then all hell is going to break loose. I plan to savor it." I glanced over and Elayne was staring at CJ.

"Elayne, this is CJ West." I inclined my head, waiting for her reaction. "She's renting the little house from Joshua Miller."

I wasn't disappointed. Elayne's eyes widened and snapped back to CJ. "Really. That's an interesting development."

I was glad that talk about the bloody wedding had promptly ended. It was going to be bad enough to relive the massacre in details the next day. I didn't want to talk about it now—or think about it. I was already dreading when my head hit the pillow later and the nightmares began.

"What do you know about the man?" I asked Elayne.

She looked over her shoulder, making sure no one was listening—some habits die hard. She slid closer to me before she answered.

"Up until the real estate, I didn't know him personally, but I *had* heard of him."

My stomach clenched in anticipation. I wasn't surprised. Even ex-Amish seemed to have a direct line to the gossip mill. "Please tell us what you know. CJ's my friend. I don't want her getting herself into a bad situation out there."

Elayne glanced at CJ, who was frozen in place, and back at me. "I guess it's been about a year since his wife drowned. When I moved away from Blood Rock, I lost contact with the community here, but I have cousins in Lancaster. I visit them every few years and we write letters. When Miranda Miller died, it was the only thing people talked about for a while, so I heard about it."

"What happened?" CJ choked out.

"It was a stormy day with heavy rains. Miranda was alone, driving her buggy over a small bridge in the southern part of the county." Elayne shook her head. "From what I was told, water was already on the bridge when she attempted to cross. It gave way when she reached the middle. She was washed down the river in the buggy. The horse managed to break free and was found in a field the following day, but Miranda wasn't so lucky. Volunteers discovered her body later that night after the rain stopped. She was floating, face down in the water."

I shivered. "That's a horrible story, but other than the usual grief involved with such an unfortunate accident, I don't see what it has to do with Joshua Miller."

Elayne frowned and lowered her voice even lower. "Because no one understood why she was out driving on that fateful day."

Playing devil's advocate for an Amish man I hardly knew and didn't even like, I spoke up, "Maybe she had to pick up supplies. A lot of people are killed in flash floods. It happens all the time."

"True." She eased back in the booth, flipping her long dark hair over her shoulder. "But she was afraid of horses—she never drove a buggy alone."

Damn. That changed everything.

25

"There must be a plausible explanation." CJ looked between me and Elayne. "My landlord couldn't have planned for a flood and bridge collapsing—could he?" The pitch of her voice rose.

I swallowed down the lump that had formed in my throat. "I'm not saying he had a hand in her death. But I've learned the hard way that the Amish have skeletons in their closets, and some of them are not very pretty." I met Elayne's frozen stare and she nodded. "Perhaps it would be better all the same if we found you another place to rent. Daniel's nearly finished renovating an apartment in the same building Elayne lives at. It might be a good fit for you."

CJ grunted and shook her head. "The farm location is perfect. I want to be away from people right now. That's why I moved all the way out here. If I wanted a flat in town, I could have stayed in Indianapolis or one of the suburbs. But that's *not* what I wanted."

I remembered CJ's stubborn streak, so I wasn't surprised. Maybe I was overreacting anyway. Joshua Miller hadn't committed any crimes that I knew of, and other than his wife's strange desire to get over her fear of horses in stormy weather, nothing seemed amiss. There was such a thing as being too paranoid, and I worried that maybe I was approaching that place.

"I guess I'll be stopping by a lot to check on you." The smile I offered CJ was a challenge.

Before CJ could argue with me about my big-sister attitude, Nancy appeared with the plates of cake and took Elayne's order. My cell phone lit up on the table.

"What are you up to?" I asked Daniel.

He ignored my question. "Are you busy right now?"

His voice sounded off and my heartrate sped up. "No, just finishing up lunch. What's going on?" I'm sure I failed at hiding my apprehension when I spoke.

"There's a situation over here at Lester Lapp's farm. Can you come out?"

"What kind of situation?"

"Ah, look—I can't talk now. Will you come?"

I hesitated. CJ was taking a bite of her cake while Elayne quietly told her about the history of Blood Rock's name.

"Sure. I'll be there soon." I hung up.

"Are you leaving?" Elayne asked.

"It was Daniel. He wants me to meet him at Lester Lapp's place."

"Is there something wrong?" She looked worried.

"I have no idea. He didn't say much at all—just that he needed me out there."

"That doesn't sound good." She smacked her lips and frowned.

"I know." I slipped my phone into my pocket. "Before I go, why don't you continue your story about Blood Rock's name?"

Elayne's eyes brightened. "Mrs. Burgsley, the town historian, told me about it. She's so ancient she might actually remember the fateful event." She chuckled and winked. "The late 1700s were pretty rough around here. The settlers were having regular run-ins with the Indians and they lived in constant fear of raids and abductions. When some criminal-cowboy types decided to take matters into their own hands, shooting up an Indian family that was down by the river, the Indians were stirred into a blood lust. It all came to a head one Sunday morning. A group of settlers were having their Sunday service up on that hill above town. Their preacher was calling out the word of God while standing on a giant boulder when the arrow pierced his heart. It's said the Indians killed twenty-six men, women and children on that day…and took scalps from them all."

I had a strong sense of déjà vu, and a conversation I'd had with Todd about the town's name flitted through my mind. I couldn't help interrupting her. "There's no giant boulder on that hill, and no documented proof about this massacre you're talking about. It's just an old wives' tale."

"Let her finish the story," CJ implored.

I shrugged and Elayne went on, "Mrs. Burgsley told me the Indians piled the bodies on the rock as a warning to anyone else who had a mind to settle in the area. Of course, more people came and they couldn't keep up with the flow of humanity. It was the Indians themselves that left, moving further west."

"What about the rock?" I spoke up.

"Mrs. Burgsley said the locals thought the blood-stained boulder was a reminder of the Indian massacre, so to rid their growing town of the gruesome memory, they dynamited it. The rocks jutting out of the river just outside of town are the remnants of that boulder. And that's where our lovely town got its name." She sipped her iced tea and grinned wickedly.

"Yeah, I've heard that story and several more." My gaze rested on CJ, who was holding her fork in front of her face. "There's no proof that a giant rock even existed, let alone got blown up," I tried to assure her.

"That's *awful*," CJ said.

"I think it's fascinating," Elayne drawled. "And so does the University of Indiana." My brows rose and Elayne elaborated without me having to ask. "Haven't you heard? They're sending a team out to investigate the story—to find evidence and prove once and for all that there was an Indian massacre here."

"Talk about the ultimate cold case." My head throbbed at the mention of the word massacre. It hit way too close to home, striking images in my head of blood-soaked white roses. I gulped down the last of my cola and stood up. "I wish them luck on that."

The sympathetic look Elayne gave me made my stomach churn in return. "What?"

"They arrive next week and Fred—" she glanced at CJ "—our mayor, wants you to escort them out to the place where it supposedly happened."

"I'm not playing tour guide to a bunch of college students on a wild goose chase. He needs to get Mrs. Burgsley out there. She's the woman they need to talk to."

"Oh, she'll be there, too." Elayne couldn't keep the grin off her face and I scowled back at her.

"Is Fred nuts? I have a lot on my plate right now."

Elayne pretended to be focused on sipping her drink. I didn't appreciate her enjoyment while I squirmed. I turned to CJ and handed her my car keys. "Why don't you stop by the grocery store down the road and pick up anything you need to stock your refrigerator. I'll meet you back at your new place later this afternoon." When she looked confused, I added, "I'll get my first deputy to drive me out there—it's no big deal. I need to talk to him anyway."

I spared only a moment more to say goodbye to Elayne and stop by Nancy's register to square up with her. By the time I went through the doorway and sunshine hit my face, my insides were tied in knots.

Todd whistled and looked my way. I couldn't see his eyes past his large shades, but the corners of his mouth were turned down.

"You've had some week, boss," he said.

I turned my attention to the passing farmland without hardly seeing it. "It feels surreal, even for me, what happened in Lancaster. In all, six innocent people celebrating a wedding died for no reason at all." I sniffed and lifted my own sunglasses to dab the corner of my eye. "I'd talked to the bride. She was a nice woman, and she was my age, which is pretty damn old for an Amish woman to be getting married." I rubbed my hands over my jeans to wipe the sweat off my palms. "Besides the obvious, you know what really upsets me?"

For a change, Todd was at a loss for words. He shrugged, keeping his eyes on the road.

"I'm suspicious that one of the reasons Miriam Coblenz never married was because she *was* in love with Brent Prowes. She wouldn't leave her people to be with him, but she couldn't bring herself to marry another, either."

"And he ended up killing her and the others. That's Shakespearian all the way," Todd said.

"Daniel says the Amish in that community will forgive the killer—they'll show grace and move on," I said absently and then pointed at the next driveway. "This is it."

Todd hit the brakes and turned in. "If it were my family or friends murdered, I wouldn't be able to forgive so easily. Maybe it makes it a little better for them since you killed the shooter. Justice was served."

"I don't think it would make any difference to them. They're a strange lot. In some ways they're hardcore—shunning for instance. Daniel's parents turned their backs on him for years because he chose to live what we'd consider a *normal* life. And yet they'd forgive a murderer. It makes little sense to me now, but perhaps someday I'll understand."

Daniel's Jeep was parked beside a white van in the driveway beside the barn. A white-capped head caught my eye in the van, but I couldn't tell who it was. Daniel and several Amish men stood in front of the barn, including Lester and Mervin Lapp and Bishop Esch. When I got out of the car, I recognized Seth Hershberger and Jerimiah Stoltzfus.

I found it difficult to breathe as I approached the group.

Jerimiah smiled when he saw me coming. "Sheriff, it's good to see you. Things were awfully confusing the other day. I wanted to say more—" he chewed on his lower lip "—but I was too upset at the time."

Seth stepped forward. "The same for me. I guess you could say we were still in shock about what had happened."

"We wanted to thank you in person for what you did for our community. You saved us," a woman's voice spoke up behind me and I whirled around.

Louise Schwartz stood beside the van. Her face was puffy and red from crying. When our eyes met, a knot formed in my throat.

I was grateful for the sunglasses when Louise came forward and wrapped her arms around me. Tears were sliding down my face too.

I patted Louise's back as she rocked against me with her soft sobs. I never could have imagined that I would form such an unfortunate bond with a girl who served me and the marshals our dinner at a restaurant.

She couldn't be more than twenty years old and she'd witnessed friends and family gunned down right before her eyes. If anyone had a right to cry, it was this girl.

"It's all right," I murmured to her. "It's over now."

She pulled back, wiping her cheeks with a handkerchief she held in her hand. "They're in heaven with our Lord Jesus…and at peace. I'm not crying for them." She sniffed and swallowed a deep breath. "My tears are for you. They told me how you climbed up into the ceiling to come to our aid—how you risked your own life to save my people."

There were hollowed out gourds hanging from a pole beside the house and purple martins flew in and out of the holes, busy with their nest building, a sure sign summer was here. As difficult as it was to fathom, life did go on for the living. We would never forget, but sunny days like this would brighten the dark memories of the wedding, burying them deeper in our minds.

"It's my job to risk my life for others—it's what I do," I said.

She shook her head vigorously. "Don't diminish your bravery. If it had been my time to go, then I would have accepted that. But I'm glad you were there and I was spared, along with my grandmother and so many others."

I worked hard to keep my emotions in check. If I began crying, I wasn't sure if I'd be able to stop any time soon. "I wish I could have saved the others—especially Miriam and her husband. It's so tragic they were killed on their wedding day."

Louise dipped her head. "They left this world as man and wife—and that's how they greeted our Father." She reached out and squeezed my shoulder.

"Our community wanted to do something special for you to show our gratitude," Jerimiah broke in, rescuing me before I broke down in front of everyone.

I turned back to the man, shaking my head. "Your visit is more than enough—really."

Jerimiah looked at Lester and then his eyes settled on Seth. "Are you sure this is a good idea?"

A smile broke out on Seth's face. "I'm fairly certain." He squeezed in between the barn doors and disappeared.

I looked to Daniel for answers, but he only shrugged and grinned.

My heart was pounding uncomfortably hard when Seth reappeared. His back was to me and he was holding something. I craned my neck to see what it was, and then I heard the little whimpering noise.

He pivoted, and in his arms was the same writhing ball of fluff that I'd held at the flea market a week earlier. My eyes bugged out and my head snapped between Daniel and Seth. "What's this?" I demanded.

"I think it's a puppy." Daniel took the squirming creature from Seth's hands and closed the distance between us. When he stopped, the puppy looked up at me with one blue eye and the other brown. Its ears poked up as though it recognized me. "I think you know this little girl personally, don't you."

"Our bishop and ministers met last night and discussed you. I was there, and I suggested that this puppy might be the perfect gift to you from our community. I saw the light in your eyes when you held her before."

I couldn't have said a word if I'd tried. My vocal chords were frozen solid. I took the puppy from Daniel and nestled it against my neck, breathing in the wonderful smell of its fur.

It took me a minute of cuddling the pup to finally find my voice. I searched Daniel's eyes. "Are you okay with having a dog? With my hectic schedule, a lot of the responsibility for her care will fall on you."

"You kidding me? I've wanted a dog for years. She's the perfect addition to our family."

His words choked me up even more. I had to take a breath and focus on the sweet bundle in my hands. *Our family.* Could we really be a family someday? This little puppy gave me hope that it was a real possibility.

Todd peeked over my shoulder. "Aww, she's precious. What are you going to call her?"

I looked up at Seth. "Does she have a name yet?"

He shook his head. "It's up to her new owner to name her."

"I'm sure you'll come up with something original," Bishop Esch chimed in, speaking for the first time.

When I looked at him, his mouth was turned up and he twirled his white beard between his fingers. I couldn't help smiling back.

"Hope. Her name is Hope," I said loudly.

"That's just the right name for her." Mervin sidled up beside me and stroked the puppy. I noticed he was wearing clean pants and a tan shirt that was buttoned up neatly. His expression was much brighter than the last time I saw him that night in the barn.

"Are you going somewhere?" I asked him.

He shrugged in a shy, yet exited way. "I get to visit Verna this weekend." He nodded towards Jerimiah and Seth. "Mother and I are sharing a ride with them on their way back to Lancaster. They're going to drop us off at the settlement in Ohio where she lives on their way through."

"Esther Lapp, Lester's wife, is my cousin. It worked out well to combine our trips," Jerimiah informed me.

All the Amish were related in some form or fashion, to the point of confusion, but seeing Mervin's smiling face made me realize how important the sense of community really was to the Plain people. Their connections to each other were what made them strong.

"Say hello to Verna for me," I said.

"I will."

"Our bishop said to tell you to consider looking for a sheriff's job in Lancaster. We need someone like you on our side," Jerimiah said.

The expression on his face was solemn. He was serious.

"Sorry, Jerimiah. You'll have to tell Matthew that we'll be keeping our sheriff here in Blood Rock," Bishop Esch spoke up in a firm voice.

I never thought I'd hear such a strong endorsement from the Amish leader. I raised my gaze to him.

"I understand you're traveling to Lancaster to finish up business there." I nodded and he continued, "I'll pray you have some boring days when you get back."

I glanced at Todd and then Daniel, thinking about the University's impending investigation of an Indian massacre that happened over two hundred years earlier and of the mystery surrounding the death of Joshua Miller's wife, and how it might affect my friend CJ.

I highly doubted the days to come would be boring.

Hope licked my chin with her rough little tongue and everyone laughed. Daniel put his arm around me and squeezed.

Tranquility was overrated. If I didn't have a mystery to solve, I'd go crazy. So I'd take one day at a time and see what the future held for me.

It wouldn't be easy, but maybe the Amish were onto something—and all I needed was a little faith.

33805060R00121

Made in the USA
Middletown, DE
27 July 2016